Part of Pip Granger's early childhood was spent in the back seat of a light aircraft as her father smuggled brandy, tobacco and books across the English Channel to be sold in 1950s Soho, where she lived above The Two Is Cafe in Old Compton Street. She travelled in Europe and Asia in the 1980s, before quitting teaching to pursue her long-cherished ambition to write. Her first novel, *Not All Tarts Are Apple*, has won the Harry Bowling Prize for fiction.

Pip Granger now lives in the West Country with her husband and pets.

www.booksattransworld.co.uk

Acclaim for
NOT ALL TARTS ARE APPLE

Not All Tarts Are Apple

PIP GRANGER

CORGI BOOKS

NOT ALL TARTS ARE APPLE
A CORGI BOOK : 0 552 14895 4

First publication in Great Britain

PRINTING HISTORY
Corgi edition published 2002

5 7 9 10 8 6 4

Copyright © Pip Granger 2002

The right of Pip Granger to be identified as the author of
this work has been asserted in accordance with sections 77
and 78 of the Copyright Designs and Patents Act 1988.

Set in 10½/15pt Sabon by
Kestrel Data, Exeter, Devon.

Corgi Books are published by Transworld Publishers,
61–63 Uxbridge Road, London W5 5SA,
a division of The Random House Group Ltd,
in Australia by Random House Australia (Pty) Ltd,
20 Alfred Street, Milsons Point, Sydney, NSW 2061, Australia,
in New Zealand by Random House New Zealand Ltd,
18 Poland Road, Glenfield, Auckland 10, New Zealand
and in South Africa by Random House (Pty) Ltd,
Endulini, 5a Jubilee Road, Parktown 2193, South Africa.

Printed and bound in Great Britain by
Cox & Wyman Ltd, Reading, Berkshire.

For my husband
Ray

Acknowledgements

My heartfelt thanks to
Jean Burnett for nagging
Jill Nicholson for listening
Nancy Norton for the computer
my agent, Jane Conway-Gordon, and my editor,
Selina Walker, for their help and advice

Not All Tarts Are Apple

1

I can't remember when I first went to live with Auntie Maggie and Uncle Bert. Rumour has it that I lived with my mum for the first few months of my life, but that she nipped into the cafe one day to borrow a few quid and somehow managed to leave without me. It seems that I have always been surrounded by the warmth of the kitchen, the smell of food cooking and the murmur of punters' voices rising and falling above the hiss and bubble of the urn.

I was blissfully unaware that Maggie and Bert were not my real mum and dad. Or at least, I knew and I didn't know, if you see what I mean. I had been at school some time before I understood that I had a real mum somewhere. It was that cow Kathy Moon who spilled the beans one day in the

11

playground. We were in the first year of the juniors by then, so I was seven. I can hear it now.

'You haven't got no proper mum and dad, you haven't,' in that slippy slimy voice she used to use. '*Your* mum's a tart.'

I didn't know what a tart was then, but I did know I didn't like that Kathy Moon saying it about my mum, whoever she was. I hit her and made her nose bleed and I didn't care.

Auntie Maggie and Uncle Bert were called up to the school but only Auntie Maggie went. Uncle Bert had to keep the cafe open and so he got Mrs Wong in to help. Auntie Maggie put on her best dress and Granny's brooch and her good shoes and took me by the hand and sailed in through the school gate like royalty. Right there in the playground she gave me a big, smacking kiss. 'Don't you worry, love. I'll sort it out. You run along and play.'

Of course, up until then I hadn't been worried at all, because I hadn't really twigged that anything was wrong, although I should have got an inkling on account of the dress and Granny's brooch. After that, though, I really was worried and tried to follow her into the building.

I suppose I was working on the theory that if I just hung on to the hem of her best moleskin coat, everything would be all right. Auntie Maggie had that effect on everyone. Just stay within the shadow of her mighty bulk and everything would be all right. Trouble was, I had competition: several dogs had followed us into the playground and were also trying to hang on to the hem of Auntie Maggie's coat. That moleskin always attracted lots of dogs. As far as I was concerned that was its charm, that and the feel of it. Of course I didn't know that hundreds of lovely little moles like the one in *The Wind in the Willows* had had to give their all to make it. Once I discovered this terrible truth, I never really felt the same about it. Anyway, I was soon shooed away and the door was slammed on several noses, including mine. I just had to wait, my apprehension growing.

The bell went and we all lined up in our classes. Miss Welbeloved (who wasn't) was on duty. This meant that we had what felt like *hours* of shuffling in our lines and putting our arms out and touching each other's shoulders to go through before she was satisfied with the precision of our spacing and the straightness of our lines and the silence of our tongues and feet. Meanwhile, the wind was whistling round that playground, turning our noses red and our knees blue. I shall never forget the rawness of that day or the agony of waiting. I had never considered the possibility of Auntie Maggie and Miss Giles, the headmistress, meeting. Now that I realized it was inevitable, I was very worried. What was worse, it had dawned on me that they would be talking about *me*.

I didn't like my worlds mixing much when I was seven. School was school and home was home. Bumping into your teacher outside school was like meeting a Martian on the bus. Martians should stay in their flying saucers, I thought, and teachers should live in cupboards with the chalk and the board rubber when not actually in use. They had no right to turn up in the greengrocer's or on the pavement outside Frenchie's like ordinary people.

Well, my auntie Maggie in school was like that. Auntie Maggie was just too big for it, and far too jolly and loud. Jolly and loud weren't encouraged in school. Screeching, yelling and laughing till you wet your knickers were just about tolerated in the play-ground or in the street but not in the school building.

Not that Auntie Maggie wet her knickers; not ever, I'll have you know. But she did laugh and shake like a jelly mountain and she had a booming voice and fingers like sausages all covered in glittering rings. Miss Giles was thin and old. She had dead straight, greying hair that she yanked sideways and anchored with enough ironmongery to sink a small ship. Her hair would not dare to fly about in wisps in the wilful way that Auntie Maggie's did. Miss Giles wore a woollen tweed skirt – always the same one – and a succession of lumpy cardigans and grey or mustard blouses the colour of sick that did up firmly at the neck and the wrists. During assembly in the school hall she sat on the stage, legs planted so far apart that we saw she wore long, pink or white directoire knickers that pinched the mean flesh above her knees in a vice-like grip. Try as I might, I could not imagine Miss Giles and my beloved auntie Maggie together.

We filed into class. I'm not sure what I was expecting to happen but I knew I was expecting something: the world to stop turning, a mighty explosion, school to disappear in a puff of smoke. What I wasn't expecting was for that two penn'orth of Gawd 'elp us, Enie Smales, to trail in with a message from Miss Giles for me and Kathy Moon to present ourselves in her office.

My heart was hammering and my knees were like jelly as we walked in silence along those cream and institution-green corridors. That wet weekend Enie was smirking. She knew trouble when she smelt it and, being merely the messenger, had the superior air of one who was not involved. I knew then why the mortality rate among messengers is said to be so high; it's to wipe that superior smirk off their chops. We arrived at the door and Kathy and I looked at each other, faces white with terror.

The scene in the office was hard to take in. Miss Giles was sitting behind her desk and Auntie Maggie was standing, red in the face. She seemed to take up all the space in the office that was not already claimed by desk, filing cabinets, bookshelves and Miss Giles. Miss Giles had shrunk and, incredible though it may seem, appeared to be cowering behind her desk. A cowering Miss Giles was a reassuring sight to me. Whatever was going on, it looked as if my auntie Maggie was on top of it.

Auntie Maggie took several deep breaths, letting them out slowly. Then she spoke. 'Rosie, you first. Tell us exactly why you belted young Kathy here and made her nose bleed. The truth now, no lies.' The last came as a bit of a surprise to me. I had never had occasion to lie to my auntie Maggie in my life. I realize now that this was because I was never really afraid of her, despite her having something of a temper. She had an enormous capacity for compassion and understanding, but of course I didn't know that then. I just knew that I never lied to her and that few people did, and if they did, she saw straight through it, so it was a waste of time anyway.

I darted a glance at Miss Giles, who seemed to have recovered a bit now Auntie Maggie's attention was elsewhere. She was sitting rigid behind her desk, eyes glittering, mouth set like a rat trap. My heart did a terrified somersault in my chest under that hard, unforgiving gaze. I turned back to the reassuring presence of Auntie Maggie and addressed myself to her. It was safer, somehow.

'We was in the playground, see, and me and Patsy and Jill was playing skipping and Kathy came up with Sandra and that and started yelling things at me so I hit her.'

Miss Giles started to speak, voice sharp like a bacon slicer. 'Whatever Kathy said, there is absolutely no excuse—'

Auntie Maggie turned a gaze on her that would have shrivelled the English Channel to a puddle. She didn't actually say, 'Shut yer gob.' She didn't have to. Miss Giles shut her gob.

Auntie Maggie turned back to me, her voice gentle. 'What did she yell at yer, luv? Don't be afraid. Speak up like a good girl. It's all right.'

I believed her. If Auntie Maggie said it was all right, then it was all right, but part of me had nagging doubts about being too explicit in front of Miss Giles. So I compromised and mumbled, 'She said I had no proper mum and dad and that me mum was a tart.'

The bacon slicer cut in again. 'How *dare* you use that word? I simply *will not* toler—' Once again she was switched off by a glare from my magnificent aunt.

Auntie Maggie turned to Kathy and in a mild tone enquired, 'And you, Kathy, do you agree with what our Rosie says? Did you say them things? The truth now, no point in lying. Seems as there was plenty of witnesses. We don't want to have to haul 'em all in, do we?'

Kathy shuffled her feet and looked at the ground. Her ears were red as she whispered, 'I never . . . I never said them things. Honest, I never.'

Indignation welled up in me. I opened my mouth to call her a liar but got no further before Auntie Maggie's voice broke in quietly but firmly. 'Be quiet, Rosie, you've had your turn. Now, Kathy, that's not really true, is it, love? There's no need to be afraid. Nobody here thinks you're bad and nobody is going to get upset, are they, Miss Giles?'

She didn't trouble to wait for a reply. 'No, nobody's going to be cross. We know that little girls don't really know about things like that. They just repeat what they've heard. *We* know that. And don't you worry, we won't ask you who told you these things. We just want to know what you said to our Rosie, that's all. Now, did you or did you not say that Rosie's mum was a tart?'

The dread word hung in the atmosphere like a fart in church; but no one dared acknowledge it and it was refusing to go away. Auntie Maggie's bejewelled sausages reached out and gently cupped Kathy's chin. She pulled the girl's scarlet face up and looked straight into her eyes. Kathy's pretty brown ones suddenly filled with tears. I watched, fascinated, as this eyeball-to-eyeball contact went on. Neither Miss Giles nor I dared to breathe as the silent messages passed between Kathy and my aunt.

At last, Kathy nodded. 'Yes, yes, I said it,' she admitted in a faint voice.

The headmistress and I breathed out noisily and Auntie Maggie beamed down at the soggy Kathy, awash with tears now. She let go of the small chin and fumbled in her bag for her handkerchief. Her voice was hearty. 'Have a good blow, dear, and wipe those pretty eyes of yours. See, it wasn't so bad, was it? Now off you go, the pair of you. What's done's done. It's time to make up and forget all about it.'

That was when Miss Giles made her big mistake. Her sharp voice cut into the cosy atmosphere Auntie Maggie had created around the three of us. 'May I remind you, Mrs Featherby, that *I* am the head here and that whatever Kathy said to Rosa' (they always called me by my real name at school) 'there is absolutely no excuse for her behaving like a barbarian in *my* school – or anywhere else, for that matter.' She turned to me. 'You, Rosa, will miss your playtimes, games and painting for the next week and let *that* be a lesson to you to keep your fists to yourself.' She turned back to Auntie Maggie. 'And can you deny that Rosa's mother's morals leave a lot to be desired?'

There was a dreadful pause as Auntie's benign expression changed to one of thunder.

Auntie Maggie looked at the headmistress, then very quietly told us to go back to class as Miss Giles and she had things to talk about. We scrambled for the door, fumbling with the knob in our haste to get out. We knew that Auntie Maggie was dangerously close to blowing and we wanted to be as far away as possible when she did.

How can adults be so stupid? Miss Giles didn't seem to see the danger as she rose to her feet with the triumphant air of one who had just wrested victory out of the jaws of defeat. The silly woman had no idea, no idea at all.

I never did find out what took place in that office after we left, although not long afterwards Miss Giles was quietly moved to a church school in a less colourful part of the borough and retired a few years later.

What did come out of it all, though, was that I had the first inkling that my safe and cosy world was not as safe as I thought, and that Maggie and Bert were not my real mum and dad.

That night, I wet the bed. I carried on wetting it, night after night. It wasn't long before Auntie Maggie woke me one morning, took in the now-familiar soggy sheets and my woebegone countenance and called a family conference.

2

It had always been my job – as soon as I was tall enough to reach it, that is – to turn the 'Closed' sign to 'Open' in the mornings. Almost as soon as the key turned in the lock, the cafe door would open and a steady trickle of early morning punters would come in for their breakfasts. Bacon, egg, fried bread, bangers, fried tomatoes and, for the discerning, fried mushrooms would flow effortlessly from Uncle Bert's hands.

Auntie Maggie stayed out front, dispensing teas, coffees, observations about the weather and an endless stream of opinions about juicy bits of local news. I would eat my breakfast at the corner table, then Auntie Maggie would leave the teas and coffees to Mrs Wong while she took me to school. Once I was safely delivered to the playground, she headed for the market and Ronnie's stall to order the day's veg.

Sometimes she would nip in and out of various shops, picking up odds and ends as she needed them. The last port of call was always the newspaper shop, where she picked up Bert's *Daily Mirror* and had a chat with old Mrs Roberts before returning to the cafe. By then the breakfast rush was over. Uncle Bert would settle down with his paper, his beloved pipe and a cuppa for a well-earned break before the dinner trade piled in.

This particular morning, however, was different. Instead of taking me to school, Auntie Maggie peeled off her flowered pinny and headed straight for the market with me in tow. The order was handed over with the minimum of civilities and we made our way briskly to the paper shop. Once back in the cafe, we settled down at the corner table to discuss my problem.

After much gentle questioning it was decided that the root of my trouble lay not so much in the knowledge that I wasn't their child – I'd always sort of known that – but that I was afraid my real mum would take me away from Maggie, Bert and the cafe just as readily as she had left me there.

Uncle Bert was a man of few words but those few

were always to the point. 'Get Sharky Finn down here, Mag. We need a word.'

Sharky Finn was the lawyer who kept a dingy office next door. His front door, painted a sad shade of green, nestled grubbily between our cafe and Mamma Campanini's delicatessen. His brass plate gleamed dully between a card boasting that Paulette gave French lessons and a sign proudly announcing that Madame Zelda was 'Clairvoyant to the Stars'.

Actually, Paulette's real name was Brenda, and she'd never been any nearer France than Wapping, while Madame Zelda also answered to Enid Fluck and was a martyr to her feet. They were regulars at the cafe.

Sharky himself was into everything. He needed to be. He had a gambling habit, a couple of mistresses and, rumour had it, a wife, two children and a mother-in-law to keep, although nobody had ever actually seen them. There wasn't a spiv in Soho that Sharky hadn't represented at one time or another when their luck ran out. He cooked books, drew up contracts – both straight and otherwise – arranged alibis and choreographed divorces in seedy hotel rooms with professional co-respondents. In short, Sharky was as bent as a two-bob watch, but clever and well qualified with it.

Now our cafe closed for nothing and nobody. It would no more have occurred to Maggie and Bert to close in order to keep an appointment with Sharky in his office than it would have occurred to Sharky to book one. When Uncle asked Auntie Maggie to get him, he did not mean to suggest for one moment that she heave her bulk up to the second floor to get him herself. It was more a suggestion that she should arrange to have it done. She cast her eye around the cafe, looking for a likely messenger. She couldn't send me because my eyes were puffy, my nose was red and I needed some earnest mopping up. Her eye lit on Luigi, Mamma Campanini's youngest son.

'Luigi, nip upstairs and ask Sharky if he would care to drop in when he's got a minute. The sooner the better, if he would be so kind.' Luigi nodded amiably and got to his feet, whistling faintly through his teeth as he strolled out to do her bidding.

While he was away I was whisked into the back of the cafe. My face was washed and a hanky produced, into which it was suggested that I 'blow good and hard'. A brush was dragged through my curls, then I was free to return to Uncle Bert's welcoming lap. I snuggled in, burrowing my face into his rough waistcoat, breathing in the familiar smell of pipe tobacco and fry-up. I was given a comforting squeeze and a large gobstopper appeared by magic from my left ear. Somehow, in hard times, Uncle Bert always seemed to magic something out of thin air or one of my ears. It could be anything: a gobstopper, a sherbet dab, a tin whistle with bright stripes or a fluorescent yo-yo. He could do other magic too, card tricks and all sorts at Christmas and family knees-ups. I was very proud of Uncle Bert's magic, and grateful too. I was contentedly slurping on the gobstopper when Sharky Finn appeared.

Auntie Maggie placed a coffee, liberally laced with brandy, in front of him. Some might think that ten in the morning was a little early to indulge in strong liquor, but Sharky wasn't one of them. He liked a drink, did Sharky, preferably one that lasted from sparrow fart to sack time. There was very little evidence of this. He rarely appeared to be drunk and the stuff never seemed to fuddle his wits during office hours, but just a hint of the wrath of grapes showed in the puffy white skin around his moist blue eyes and the tiny broken veins that darted across cheekbones and hooter.

He took a good swig of the coffee, struck a match and lit the stub of cigar that hung from his lip. The blue, aromatic smoke drifted around his sparse blond hair on its way to the ceiling. He let out a deep sigh of satisfaction and tipped his chair back before he spoke. 'You called and, as you can see, I came. What can I do for you good people, hm?'

Uncle Bert took charge, an unusual occurrence in our household but not unheard of. 'It's our Rosie. As you know, Sharky, she has lived with us ever since she was bollock high to our Tom' (this was a reference to our lace-eared old cat who patrolled the cafe and its surroundings) 'but it's always been a sort of loose arrangement.'

Uncle Bert continued to outline the problem: namely, the sudden realization by all parties concerned, with the possible exception of my real mum who was probably 'too Brahms to give a monkey's', that our situation was far from satisfactory, and that it was seriously upsetting not only 'the rug-rat' (me) but everyone else. 'We've got used to her, like, and anyway we need her to see to the signs and that.' He gave me another reassuring squeeze.

'We don't reckon we could part with her now. So, you see, Sharky, it's time we did something about it. We've decided to check it out with you and see if you have any suggestions.'

Sharky had been listening carefully without interruption and now there was a long pause as he pulled on his dead cigar and stared at the ceiling. Everyone waited in silence for his answer: our little group at the corner table, the punters, who had long since given up all pretence of not listening, and Mrs Wong. At last he seemed to reach some sort of conclusion. He tipped forward until all four legs of his chair were on the floor and looked meaningfully at his empty coffee cup. Mrs Wong glided over to refill it, brandy and all. He took an appreciative slurp, coughed and spoke.

'It seems to me,' he said slowly, 'that you need some kind of adoption agreement that will hold up in court if it ever comes to that. Also, of course, you will have to get her mother to sign it, in front of witnesses, preferably me and one or two others. I can start drawing up the agreement, if you like, ready for when she next blows in, assuming it's not in the next day or so. Do you reckon she'll play ball and sign the thing?'

All eyes in the place turned to Auntie Maggie and Uncle Bert.

'I reckon, if she's sober enough to write but Brahms enough to be amiable,' Uncle Bert said. 'That'll be the hard bit, getting her in just the right frame of mind. Best get the agreement written and then we can put the word out for her to show up here. The little 'un likely won't settle till it's in the bag and neither will Mag. Will you, love?'

Auntie Maggie shook her head, eyes moist. She heaved a great sigh and lumbered heavily to her feet. 'Well, this ain't getting no baby bathed, is it? Time you was in the kitchen, Bert, limbering up for dinner. Thanks, Sharky. If you could get them papers ready, quick as you like, we'd be grateful.'

She turned to me, eyes soft. 'Now, what do you want to do, young lady? Stay for dinner and back to school? Or help your auntie Maggie for the afternoon?'

Of course, there was no contest: I opted to stay put and help. With that, the little party at the corner table broke up, Uncle Bert headed for his kitchen, Sharky took the last gulp from his coffee cup and made for the door, and Auntie Maggie asked Mrs Wong to hold the fort while we went upstairs for 'a bit of a chat'.

The 'bit of a chat' made me feel tons better. My auntie Maggie told me how much she and Bert loved me and how they had come to rely on me being there every day. She explained how much she had always wanted a little girl but how, somehow, she and Bert had not been 'blessed' and then I had come along and made everything all right.

29

Then she asked me if I wanted to ask her anything, anything at all. Of course, at the time I couldn't think of anything much, I was too busy revelling in the warmth of her cuddles and the smell of her as I buried my nose in her ample bosom. Auntie Maggie had a smell all of her own; a warm smell with a hint of face powder and soap. I was snuggled up in her lap for a long time, thumb in mouth, basking in the comfort of it while she talked.

She told me all about the day I came to stay, near Christmas. She explained how she and Bert hadn't been expecting me, how they had had to borrow nappies, bottles and food from one of Mamma Campanini's brood to see us over the first night and how I had slept in a drawer. She told me how she and I had had a lovely time hunting around for clothing coupons and baby clothes. She told me how Mamma Campanini's lot had had a whip-round and had come up with a cot, a pram, toys and loads of clothes. I asked what happened to it all and she explained that once I grew out of it, it went back to the Campanini tribe for the next new baby.

She also told me all about the big knees-up held in the cafe to welcome me in, once we'd all settled down a bit and got used to things. How Paulette, Madame Zelda, Mamma and Papa Campanini, their kids and their kids' kids, Mrs Roberts, Ronnie from the market and his missis, and Sharky and loads of others had all come and brought me things. Being a greedy little bugger and wanting to prolong this lap-time, I demanded a list of everything and who brought it. Amazingly enough, Auntie Maggie remembered it all, or at least she pretended to.

By the time she had reeled off the complete list, I had gathered my wits a bit and thought to ask about my real mum. That was when I realized that the woman I always thought of as 'the Perfumed Lady' was, in fact, my mother. She visited the cafe now and then and sometimes she brought me presents. I liked her. She laughed a lot and wore princess clothes. She would bring me wonderful things like silver shoes, glittery jewellery to dress up in and satin ribbons. I thought she was a Fairy Godmother. Sometimes, though, she would sort of blubber over me and call me her baby and try to cuddle me too hard. I didn't like that and would get frightened and hide behind Maggie or climb on to Bert's lap.

I had just about had time to take all this in when Mrs Wong appeared in the doorway to ask if Auntie Maggie could lend a hand with the dinners. I was left feeling that all the worry of the past few weeks had been a waste of time. Now I knew who she was, I realized that my mum wouldn't try to hurt me. Everything was going to be fine.

Uncle Bert, Auntie Maggie and Sharky had it all under control.

3

Life for me carried on pretty much as before. Sharky kept his promise and wrote up an agreement and delivered it to Uncle Bert, and word was sent out to find the Perfumed Lady.

The news network in our bit of London was far more efficient than the wireless or the post office. Paulette asked among her colleagues and their pimps, and Sharky made enquiries in his circle of gamblers and clients. Madame Zelda gazed into her crystal ball in the hope of catching a glimpse of her. When that failed, she also took the precaution of mentioning it to the steady stream of theatrical hopefuls who came looking for a sign of their big break. Buskers scanned theatre and cinema queues looking for 'faces' to pass the whisper to and soon the message had travelled to every nook and cranny in the manor. There wasn't a pub or club in Soho that didn't know that the Perfumed Lady was wanted at the cafe. We even informed the police, not a common occurrence round our way. But T.C. was different. He was liked by us all and considered straight and fair-minded. He had the most gorgeous, crinkly blue eyes and Auntie Maggie said that his hair would have curled if only the police force would let it grow long enough. But they wouldn't. They had rules about that sort of thing, even for plain-clothes officers like him.

Days turned into weeks and still she didn't show. No one had seen her. This wasn't really surprising; she led an erratic sort of life, and for all anyone knew she could be abroad with one of her posh punters or be taking a rest anywhere in the country. Sometimes things got a little warm for a girl and she might take herself up to Leeds, Manchester or even Scotland for a whiff of healthier air until the heat turned down. After all, a change was as good as a rest, and a brass could trade anywhere where there were men.

Still, despite the waiting, I was feeling a lot better. I stopped wetting the bed. I was much relieved that we had a plan, even if I was a little hazy as to what this was. I had absolute faith that Auntie Maggie,

Uncle Bert and Sharky would get it sorted. Kids are like that, aren't they? It never occurs to them that there are just some things that grown-ups cannot do. I still remember the shock the first time Uncle Bert couldn't mend one of my toys. I took it to Auntie Maggie, sure that she would work the miracle, and was staggered when she couldn't either. The world as I knew it took a real shunt. Then I managed to convince myself that the failure was a one-off, a glitch in the works; that it was all a big mistake. I did such a good job that I had to go through the whole thing again later. It was like realizing the Queen had a bum; very weird, believe me.

Luckily, at this stage, the awful knowledge that my auntie Maggie and uncle Bert were fallible had not crossed my mind, so I was happy. Weekdays, I went to school as usual and on Saturdays I 'helped' in the cafe. My 'helping' was largely confined to wiping down tables and chatting to the regulars. Saturdays and after school were profitable times for me. There were not that many children actually living in the area even in those days, and small girls with blond curls and big blue eyes were IN at the time, what with the coming Coronation and all, and Princess Anne being so popular. Everyone thought I looked just like her, which cheesed me off more than a bit, seeing that I was three years older than she was. It was a regular occurrence for me to have pennies, threepenny bits and sixpences thrust upon me. I was even stopped in the street when I was out with Auntie Maggie or Uncle Bert. I had quite a thriving little business going. As the weeks passed and my mum still hadn't showed, the regulars began to feel sorry for me and my piggy bank bulged.

I realize now that the waiting must have been hard on Auntie Maggie and Uncle Bert, but they didn't show it. As far as I was concerned, life was following its regular pattern. After school, I had my tea at the corner table and then helped to close the cafe for the night. This was a complicated business that began with me turning the sign from 'Open' to 'Closed', and Auntie Maggie pulling the blind down over the glass door. Left-over counter food such as cakes and biscuits were sampled and sorted into 'still fresh' and 'past it'. The 'still fresh' went into tins, and the 'past its' were set aside as the basis of trifles and other puddings. Old bread became bread pudding, dark and rich with spices and dried fruit and lip-smackingly delicious. I really loved the crusty bits at the corners of the baking tin and it was my treat to prise these loose and munch them.

The rest would take hours. Salt, pepper and

vinegar shakers were collected and refilled, using little funnels, one for each job. I was kept well away from the pepper as I tended to get it all over the place, including up my nose and in my eyes. Smelly ashtrays were emptied and washed, the tables were wiped down, chairs lifted on to them, and the floor was swept and scrubbed.

Uncle Bert cleared and scrubbed down the decks in the kitchen, ready for the baking of the next day's puddings and pies. He also sorted his leftovers. The stuff that was still good was put to one side for one or two down-and-outs that he fed at the back door. Uncle Bert never turned away a tramp, on the principle of 'there but for the grace of Gawd and my good woman go I'. The rest was binned. Washing up of plates, cutlery and cups and saucers was done all day by whoever was free to do it. There was a sink behind the counter and drying racks suspended over the draining boards. Auntie Maggie, Mrs Wong and Uncle Bert all did a bit. However, the end of the day was when the heavy stuff, cooker, pots, pans and baking tins, had to be scoured and scrubbed. This took elbow grease, and Auntie Maggie, Mrs Wong and Uncle Bert were all far too busy to see to it, so Ernie came after closing to get stuck in. He arrived as Mrs Wong left.

The changeover was my cue to get ready for bed. Auntie Maggie would see Mrs Wong out at about sixish and then I would be whisked upstairs for a bath and a cup of Ovaltine, then bed and a bedtime song or story, depending on Auntie Maggie's mood or my pleading. Uncle Bert would come up and tuck me in with a goodnight kiss to end my day. God knows when theirs ended. The smell of bread pudding would waft up the stairs long after I was tucked in.

4

It was late on one wet and windy night towards the end of April that I heard a loud hammering at the cafe door. I had been curled up in bed all snug and warm with my teddy for hours when the row woke me. The stairs creaked loudly and Uncle Bert's voice was raised in irritation. 'Hang about, hang about, keep your hair on, I'm coming. No need to wake the bleeding dead, is there?'

There was a rattling noise as the key was turned in the lock and the bolts, top and bottom, were drawn. 'Bugger me, look what the cat's dragged in.' Uncle Bert's voice was muffled but I could hear him through my bedroom door. 'We've been hanging about like spare pricks at a wedding waiting for you. Well, don't just stand there dripping like a drowned wassname. Get your arse in here.

'Mags! Get yourself down here and see what the tide's washed up. Her ladyship has finally showed her face and as pissed as a newt, if I'm any judge.'

Next came the heavy thud of Auntie Maggie's tread on the stairs and then a loud exclamation. 'Oh my Gawd, look at the state of you! Get them wet things off straight away. Bert, you put the kettle on and make some strong coffee, there's a love. Looks as if she could do with something hot and sobering. I'll find a towel and a dressing gown. No, dear, don't get undressed right there in front of the windows. Don't want to give them buggers out there a free show now, do we? Take her in the kitchen, Bert, and I'll get them dry things.'

More slow thuds and then a creak as my bedroom door opened and Auntie Maggie peered silently in. I decided it was best if I pretended sleep and made my breathing slow and deep. I heard a muttered 'Good', and the door closed.

Next thing I knew, it was a bright, shiny morning and Auntie Maggie stood beaming beside my bed.

'Wakey-wakey, rise and shine. Time you was getting up, my girl. It's Saturday, no school today and I need your help this morning.'

I was up and dressed in very short order, stopping only for a lick and a promise on the way. I knew something was up and vague memories of the late night rumpus were coming back to me. However, if I had hopes of seeing the visitor, I was disappointed. There was no sign of her.

The Saturday morning routine carried on as normal. Uncle Bert was already in his kitchen, getting ready for the breakfast trade, Auntie Maggie had the urn going and my breakfast was waiting for me on the corner table. I skipped to the cafe door to perform the morning ritual with the signs. Auntie Maggie shot the bolts and I turned the key.

The first customer that morning was Luigi Campanini, not so much an early riser as a late to bedder. In an attempt to mend his wicked ways, Mamma Campanini had a tendency to lock the door on him if he was out late at night. Of course, this fazed Luigi not at all; he just camped out somewhere much more undesirable until the morning. If he was in the money, he hung out at a club or at a poker game. If he was broke, he merely called on one of his many female admirers and put up there for a night. Luigi had no shortage of admirers.

He strolled into the cafe, whistling through his

teeth. Luigi's teeth were lovely, I thought, as they looked white and strong against his dark skin. According to my teacher, Italians were Mediterranean types and they often had dark skin which helped guard against getting sunburn in their hot summers. 'Olive', she called it. Olive suited Luigi, and not just because it showed off his gnashers. It went with his large brown eyes and glossy black hair.

'Morning, Bert, Maggie, Shorty.' (That was me.) 'How you diddling? Give us the usual and a coffee to be getting on with.' He flipped me a two-bob bit. 'Run across and get me a *Mirror*, Shorty, and buy yourself a sherbet dab or something.'

'You ain't goin' nowhere, young lady, till you've got yourself on the outside of that breakfast. Morning, Luigi.' Auntie Maggie changed tack. 'Out on the razzle again last night? Coffee coming up.'

Luigi sat at his favourite table by the window. He liked to keep an eye on things. 'Has wassname turned up here yet?' He indicated me with a nod of his head and a conspiratorial roll of the eyes. 'I saw her last night in Frenchie's with some geezer. She'd had a few, but I told her you was looking for her and she said she'd heard and that she'd look in later.'

Auntie Maggie made her way to his table, coffee cup gripped in one hand, a plate of bread and butter in the other. She placed them carefully on the table in front of him and sat down opposite.

'Yes, we seen her. Matter of fact she's sleeping it off upstairs. Couldn't get much sense out of her, to be honest. She wasn't in any state to talk things over. I doubt if she knew who she was, let alone being able to see or hold a pen. We thought we'd have a go today, when she comes round. You reckon you could ask your mum and dad to do the necessary if we need witnesses?'

I listened carefully as I munched my egg, bacon, fried slice and tomatoes and slurped my milk in the corner. So it *was* my mum who came last night. My stomach lurched as all my insecurities came flooding back. Suppose she wouldn't sign the paper? Say she dragged me away with her and I never saw Auntie Maggie and Uncle Bert again? I slunk over to where Auntie Maggie was sitting and clamped myself to her side.

Her beefy arm wrapped itself around me and gave me a squeeze. 'Don't you worry, love. It'll be all right. You nip across now and get Luigi's paper and your dab. Be careful of that road and don't hang about. Come straight back here.'

When I got back with Luigi's paper, the cafe had filled up a bit. There were a few strangers who had obviously sampled the nightlife of the West End a little too enthusiastically the night before and were nursing hangovers and empty wallets. You could always recognize them: they tottered in gingerly, wincing at every sound and they had to search their pockets very, very carefully to find the price of a cup of tea. Sometimes they couldn't scrape it together but if Maggie liked the look of them, she let them have it on the house.

Paulette and Madame Zelda were settled over steaming cups of tea at a table next to Luigi's. They stopped talking abruptly as I joined the little group, paper clutched in one hand, dab and change in the other, then resumed their conversation quietly, on account of the strangers. There was an air of tension about the place as we waited for my mum to put in an appearance. Discussion of possible strategies had been exhausted and it was agreed that we could only wait and see.

'Anyone know where Sharky is?' Auntie Maggie asked the assembled company as she arrived with a tray of fresh teas, coffee and a glass of milk for me. 'We could do with him here when she gets down.'

There were several theories as to the possible whereabouts of Sharky. One was that he was sleeping it off somewhere, another was that he was still in the clutches of an all-night card game. One thing was certain: he wouldn't be at home, wherever that was, not on a Saturday morning. Friday nights were far too good to waste in front of the fire, listening to the wireless.

Paulette was just running through a list of possibilities when everyone's head turned to the back of the cafe. We were all suddenly aware of the dishevelled figure framed in the doorway that led to the flat above. Her long blond hair was all over the place, and under the smeared make-up left over from the night before her skin had a green pallor between a mass of bruises. She was wrapped up in what looked like a bedspread, her feet were bare and her voice was husky and cracked.

'Has anyone got a hair of the bastard that bit me, and a fag?' The Perfumed Lady's hand shook as she pushed a lock of hair away from her swollen eyes.

Maggie's voice was gentle as she rose from her seat at the table. 'Morning, love. Let's get you back upstairs and find you a dressing gown. Then we can think about breakfast and seeing to that face of yours. You look as if you've been run over by a train.' We heard Maggie's voice coaxing softly as they disappeared up the stairs. 'Come on now, dear, up we go. That's it, gently does it. Here's the cotton wool and witch hazel – you're not cut, so it shouldn't sting. There! That's better. Now I think we've still got a drop of brandy in the cupboard and there's some fags in the drawer.'

We were still staring at the empty doorway when Uncle Bert appeared from his kitchen, wiping his hands on his apron. As I said, the cafe closed for nothing and nobody, so you can imagine my shock when Uncle Bert started to shoo everyone out. That, more than anything, showed the gravity of the situation, and I was afraid.

'Right folks, we got business to attend to, so if you would kindly finish up as quick as you can I'll close the caff and get stuck in. Luigi, could you put the word out for Sharky to show up here as soon as possible? Paulette and Madame Zelda, could you keep your eyes peeled and all? Mind you, judging by the state of her this morning, it'll take a while to get her in any condition to line up behind her eyes, let alone attend to what's being said. Has anyone got any brandy, or vodka maybe? We only had a drop left after Sharky gave it a bashing and it looks as if she'll need a bit to settle her guts and stop the shakes.'

'I got a bottle of brandy next door you can have,' Madame Zelda spoke up. 'Purely medicinal, of course. I 'spect Paulette's got some too for that pimp of hers, haven't you, Paulette?'

Paulette nodded cautiously. 'Yes, I got some malt whisky but I'd better keep a bit by in case Dave comes. You know what 'e's like when he wants something and I 'aven't got it.' Her eyes held a funny expression that I didn't understand.

No one liked Dave. He was a runt of a man, dark with bright, glittering blue eyes that darted this way and that. He was restless and given to knocking Paulette and his other tarts about just for the hell of it. He was 'a greedy little sod' as my auntie Maggie put it. Even then I understood that he wanted things, did Dave, and plenty of them – flash clothes, enough gold tom to stock H. Samuel's and a motor, but he didn't want to work to get them. Oh no! He had a string of girls 'who worked their arses off' for that. Funny what you remember. I can still hear the bitterness in their voices whenever Auntie Maggie and Madame Zelda talked about him. They hated pimps, especially Dave, but we all liked Paulette.

Everyone trailed out. The casual punters were encouraged to hurry up and go, Luigi went in search of Sharky, Paulette and Madame Zelda went next door to find their contributions of booze, and I went with them to bring the bottles down.

5

I loved Paulette's rooms and would use any excuse to go up to see her. There were mirrors everywhere, even on the ceiling in her bedroom. There were frills and fringes and satin all over the place. The air smelt of smoke and Evening in Paris.

The really special thrill came when she let me dress up. Both of us would get wildly excited as we turned over drawers and rummaged in the wardrobe looking for *the* outfit. Once dressed in one of her satin dressing gowns or a frilly petticoat, with a pair of gold stilettos engulfing my tiny feet, I would search through boxes and drawers looking for the right jewels. Long dangly earrings would soon glitter at my earlobes, bright bangles would adorn my upper arms and ropes of twinkling beads or fake pearls would be wound around my neck.

Next, I would perch on the little gilt and velvet chair in her bedroom and she would make me up. On would go powder, rouge, eye shadow, lipstick and, as finishing touches, an eyebrow pencil 'beauty spot' and a liberal dousing of perfume. Then I would strut my stuff with a wobbling, mincing step and put on an impromptu show for her. She would clap and laugh and yell 'Bravo!' and 'More, more!'

Sometimes, if things were slack, Madame Zelda and Sharky joined my audience. At Christmas and birthdays I was whisked up to Paulette's rooms and dressed, ready to give a command performance for Auntie Maggie, Uncle Bert and everyone at the knees-up in the cafe. I have always been a terrible show-off.

It would take what felt like hours of Auntie Maggie's scrubbing and tutting to get me clean after one of these sessions, but it was worth it. Still, on this particular Saturday the mood was sombre and tense and even I realized that dressing up was out of the question. Paulette solemnly decanted some of Dave's precious whisky into a spare bottle.

Impulsively she bent down and hugged and kissed me. 'Good luck, sweetheart. It'll be OK, you'll see.'

The next stop was Madame Zelda's place to pick up the brandy. Her flat was identical in layout to Paulette's but two floors down, Sharky's office being wedged between the two apartments. Madame Zelda's consulting room was almost as good as Paulette's as far as I was concerned, but in an entirely different way. Madame Zelda went in for drama and plenty of velvet. The walls were stiff with moons, stars and astrological symbols painted in gold. But my two favourite things were the endless caches of sweets in coloured glass bowls that crowded every surface and the stuffed, moth-eaten monkey that climbed the standard lamp, whom I loved. The light was always dim in there and the sweet smell of incense warred with the heavily medicinal smell of Madame Zelda's foot cream.

Madame Zelda carried one of the bottles down for me. The stairs were dark and steep and the front-door lock was high. She saw me to the door of the cafe, which was now closed, and waited with me until our knock was answered by Uncle Bert.

'Do you want me to look after the little 'un, Bert?' she asked. 'I can always take her to the cartoons in Piccadilly Circus if you like.'

Uncle Bert stepped back to let us in and relieved us of our respective bottles. 'Hang on a tick, I'll ask.'

We waited in silence and listened to his footsteps

on the stairs and the murmur of voices. Then we heard his footsteps again, coming closer this time.

'Maggie says that would be very kind, Madame Zelda, very kind indeed. P'raps you could give us a couple of hours to get her ladyship cleaned up a bit and to settle her stomach. She's heaving at the minute. Not nice for the kid to see that.' He turned to me. 'You go with Madame Zelda, Rosie, and see some cartoons. Her ladyship should be feeling a bit better in an hour or two.'

We stuck our heads in next door to yell up the stairs to Paulette to ask if she wanted to come. She did, so we waited for a bit until she was ready and then we walked round to Piccadilly Circus.

I was worried about what was happening at home. Maybe Auntie Maggie and Uncle Bert wouldn't be able to get the Perfumed Lady to sign. Would she take me away with her? I didn't want to go. I wanted to stay where it was safe and familiar. I wanted Auntie Maggie. I was so miserable the cartoons were a blur, and it didn't even occur to me to wonder where Paulette disappeared to in the middle and why she was counting money when she came back.

By the time we got back to the cafe, Auntie Maggie, Uncle Bert, Luigi and a rumpled Sharky were gathered round the corner table. Nobody appeared to be speaking as Madame Zelda rapped on the cafe door to get their attention. They all glanced towards us and Auntie Maggie got up heavily and waddled across the room.

Once she got the door open, she took one look at my face and gathered me into her arms. Oh, the relief of it! All the tension seemed to leave me as I melted into that soft bosom and got a whiff of her familiar Auntie Maggie smell. I began to cry as she carried me to the table and set me down gently. I clambered on to her lap and the only sound was the odd sob that escaped around the thumb in my mouth. Paulette and Madame Zelda pulled up some chairs and joined the group.

The sound of the toilet being flushed drifted down to us, footsteps sounded on the stairs and the Perfumed Lady appeared in the doorway and walked across to the table. She sat down. She was dressed now, her hair was brushed and there had been some attempt at make-up, but her eyes were still black and puffy. Her lovely clothes had been pressed but nothing could disguise the fact that they were torn in places. As her long fingers wrapped themselves around a glass of brandy, I noticed that her red nail polish was badly chipped and her glass shook. She took a long gulp and looked at me above the rim of her glass. Her lovely eyes filled with tears. She set her glass down among the cups, plates, bottles and the brimming ashtray, reached across and gently stroked my hair.

'So, sweetheart, I understand you have been upset, and that you are afraid that I will come and take you away with me? Would that be such a *terrible* thing?' Her voice was husky and sad. She didn't wait for an answer, but carried on talking as if there was no one else in the room, just her and me.

'Yes, I suppose it would be. Cruel, really, after all these years. You're happy here. I know you're happy here and that is all that really matters.' At this, the tears that had been welling up slowly spilled over her lower lids and ran down her face. She made no attempt to wipe them away, as they gathered under her small, pointed chin and dripped on to the table and got lost among the clutter. She let her hand fall from my hair and took another gulp of her brandy.

'Sharky, have you got that agreement?' She seemed to be having trouble breathing and her voice grew harsher. 'Better get it over with, before I change my mind and convince myself the poor little sod can save me. I'm not the stuff of which decent mothers are made. God knows, I should know that. I can't even look after myself.'

She reached over and took the paper and the pen that Sharky offered. Madame Zelda cleared her a space on the table, and she began to read the paper silently, tears dripping steadily on to it, smudging the ink. When she finished she looked first at Sharky, then at Auntie Maggie and Uncle Bert and then at me.

'I will be able to see her though, won't I, Maggie, Bert? You'll let me see her from time to time, won't you?' She was pleading, and her voice, which had changed again, was almost too soft to hear.

'Of course, love. Of course you will see her. Nothing'll change. It'll be just the same as it's always been. This is only to make Rosie feel more settled, like. Not to hurt you. We don't want to hurt you, do we, Mags?'

I felt Auntie Maggie nodding vigorously and looked up to see that she was crying too. 'You have my word on it,' she said, and then let out a loud tearing sob and squeezed me hard.

With shaking fingers the Perfumed Lady signed and, almost before her hand had finished moving, Sharky had whipped the sheet of paper away and flourished some more.

'Sign these two as well. They're copies. Maggie, Bert, you sign too, and then Paulette and Madame Zelda can be witnesses. Luigi, you're too young, not being twenty-one yet.'

Everyone was busy writing and Luigi got up and ambled over to the counter and fetched some clean glasses. He sloshed some fizzy orange into one and brought them all over on a tray and poured the last of the brandy into the rest. Then he walked round the table and put his arm around my mother. She turned her face into his narrow chest and, like Auntie Maggie, began to sob loudly. He held her for a long time while we all watched silently, then when at last the crying slowed and finally stopped he patted her gently on the back and fished out a snowy white handkerchief from his pocket.

'Here you are, love, have a good blow and a good wipe round. You know you've done the right thing for Shorty and for you. Drink up, you'll feel better. Shorty, pass the drinks round. It's like a bleeding morgue in here.'

Everyone seemed to let out great shuddering sighs, and Madame Zelda, Paulette, Auntie Maggie and Uncle Bert all wiped their eyes, joined in an orgy of nose blowing and settled down with their drinks.

Madame Zelda's voice broke the silence. 'You'll

never guess – Paulette only went for a quick knee-trembler with one of her reglars right in the middle of Mickey Mouse. Shoulda bin Donald Duck if you arst me.'

The room exploded into hysterical laughter and the tension vanished.

Paulette spluttered into her drink, her face red as she shrieked, 'Ooh, you sod, Madame Zelda. Fancy letting out my trade secrets like that. Anyway, you shouldn't talk so dirty in front of little Rosie here.'

6

I had a lot of trouble thinking of the Perfumed Lady as 'my mum'. To me, she was and still is the Perfumed Lady. That's how I first thought of her when she was merely a mysterious person who popped up now and then, and that's how she stayed. She would arrive unexpectedly, bearing gifts or wanting money, and then disappear again to God knows where. Her life and the people in it were a complete mystery to me. Perhaps I was too young, but discovering that she was my real mother didn't really change how I felt about her. She was still the Perfumed Lady, nothing much to do with me, she was like a distant aunt, kind enough when she thought about it but not all that interested in kids.

She stayed with us for quite a while after that Saturday when she signed me over. I suppose she was recovering a bit before she faced the world again. The bruises needed to fade and her liver needed a break too. To begin with, even though we were under the same roof, I didn't see that much of her. She was still in bed when I left for school and when I got back she'd be lounging about upstairs, painting her fingernails, taking long baths or reading. She spent a lot of time reading. I thought it was a very funny thing for her to be doing. No one I knew read actual *books*. Sometimes Paulette flipped through a magazine in a bored fashion or Madame Zelda pored busily over an almanac and sucked her teeth. Uncle Bert read his paper when he got the chance and Auntie Maggie might look at it when he had finished, but no one read *books*, except teachers of course and maybe the odd punter at the cafe. As I got to know her better, I found that books were a real passion with her. She always had one in her bag or pocket.

The happiest memories I have of the Perfumed Lady were of the trips we used to take to the Charing Cross Road, which began on that visit and continued ever after. I got in from school one day and she announced that she and I were going out. She could hardly wait for me to have a biscuit and a glass of milk, and was dancing from foot to foot as she watched me finish the last gulp. A quick wipe at my moustache and we were off. I tried to get her to tell me where we were going but all she would say was 'Wait and see.' So I waited and saw and you could have knocked me down with a feather when we got there.

We turned right out of the cafe and walked down the street at a fair old clip so that I had to skip and run to keep up with her. We swept into Greek Street and made our way through Soho Square and we didn't even stop for me to peer in at the windows of the little house. At the top of the square we turned right into Sutton Row and came out at the top end of Charing Cross Road. We crossed over and dived into the entrance of the first bookshop we came to.

It was dark and musty and seemed to go on for ever. There were bookshelves from floor to ceiling and these funny step things with a banister and wheels that you could climb up on to get books from the top shelves. The first time we went I was too shy to explore the possibilities of this contraption, but on later visits I had a wonderful time climbing all over them and whizzing up and down the aisles. There were trestle tables on the pavement outside with boxes of bargain books and inside, every conceivable surface held a precarious pile of volumes.

They were stacked on the floor, on chairs and on desks as well as on the shelves. It was a treasure trove, although I didn't realize that the first time we went. I was too overawed by the strangeness of it all. I had never been in a bookshop before, or a library for that matter, and didn't know what to expect.

As we pushed the door open, a little brass bell on an elegantly curved arm tinkled and a figure appeared at the back of the shop. He was small and grey and very, very round. He wore a waistcoat with a heavy gold chain stretched across his ample belly and his hair stuck out at all angles around his head like a grey halo. He had the face of an elderly child, round and innocent with smooth red cheeks. He smiled an enormous smile of recognition and his arms stretched out in front of him in a gesture of uninhibited welcome.

'Cassandra, my dear, it has been such a long time. Where have you been?'

I looked behind us, wondering who this Cassandra was.

'I have all the books you wanted, tucked away safely in the back,' the gnome continued. 'And who is this little lady, hm?' His shaggy eyebrows shot up to emphasize the question.

'Hello, Mr Herbert. How nice to see you again.'

My mother towered over the delighted little man. 'This is Rosa and she desperately needs some books.'

'Does she indeed? And what sort of books do you desperately need, Rosa?'

Of course I was too bewildered to answer. One, I wasn't aware of my desperation and two, who the hell was this Cassandra person? I had heard my mum referred to as all sorts of things – 'that tart', 'her ladyship', 'the Perfumed Lady', 'dear', 'love', 'ducks', 'her mum', 'Rosa's mother', and 'that piss artist' to name but a few – but never *Cassandra*.

However, it seemed that Mr Herbert and my mum didn't really need me to help. They got busy discussing books and I just sort of lurked, taking it all in. Mysterious words like *'Borrowers'*, *'Railway Children'* and *'Pigeon Post'* were bandied about, along with 'Perhaps a little young' and 'No, no one is likely to read them to her, unless I'm there of course.' They wandered off and started to delve here and there and after a while they emerged with a modest pile.

There were other treats in store over the next few days, weeks and months. Even after she left the cafe, the Perfumed Lady would suddenly appear and whisk me off somewhere. One Saturday she took me to the Natural History Museum and I fell in love with dinosaurs. Another time she took me to see the Egyptian mummies at the British Museum and I fell in love with Egypt. We pored over the lovely clothes at the Victoria and Albert Museum, and naturally all these discoveries and love affairs had to be accompanied by the right books, which meant lots and lots of visits to Mr Herbert.

As it turned out, the Perfumed Lady was wrong about people not reading to me. Once I had a small library of my own, Auntie Maggie and Uncle Bert got into the habit of reading to me if the books were too difficult, and sometimes even if they weren't. We all enjoyed discovering the new worlds between those battered and dusty covers. Uncle Bert liked the adventure stories best, and Auntie Maggie liked everything. They took it in turns to read, but whenever possible the three of us would curl up together and share the magic. At weekends, Uncle Bert would launch into *Treasure Island*, *Pigeon Post* or some other rip-roaring tale of adventure, displaying an unsuspected talent for reading aloud and entering into the spirit of the thing. All the characters had their own voices and if you closed your eyes you could just see them all. Auntie Maggie and I would listen, enraptured, to these stories of derring-do.

My favourites changed with each new discovery,

but if I was to pick one book from that time it would be *The Wind in the Willows*. We were to read it many times over the years but it was the special book that the Perfumed Lady and I shared during the weeks she stayed. Each night, after my bath, she would read me the adventures of Toad, Ratty, Mole and Mr Badger as I lay warm and tired in my bed. Sometimes Maggie or Bert would slip in and listen to the tales of the river bank until sleep overcame me and I was tucked in and kissed goodnight.

7

I remember that last evening when the Perfumed Lady left the cafe and went back to her own life. It was a Sunday, the street outside was quiet and I had had my bath. I was in my nightie and we had all gathered for our nightly episode of *The Wind in the Willows*.

It was a bit snug in my room for all of us, but we managed. I was curled up in a corner of my bed, tight against the wall, so that there was room for the Perfumed Lady to sit beside me; I liked to look at the pictures as she read. Uncle Bert was perched on the end of the bed and Auntie Maggie had possession of the only chair.

The window was open and a light breeze occasionally lifted the curtains. I liked my summer curtains, which had clusters of pink roses tied with blue bows dotted about on a white background. I liked my winter ones too, which were old and made of a soft, faded pink velvet heavy enough to keep out the bitter draughts. They were nice to stroke; you could make patterns with your fingers by brushing the pile this way and that. I loved the summer ones best, though, because I chose them and because I liked to try and count the posies. I always fell asleep before I had managed to count them all.

Anyway, we were all in my room listening to the soft, well-educated tones of the Perfumed Lady as she read to us. She got to the very last page of the big green book, read the bit about how fond Mr Badger was of children and then snapped the covers shut with an air of finality. She closed her eyes and leaned back against the wall with the book in her hands. She sighed.

'Well, that's the end of that. Now we've finished it, it's about time I got back to my own place and earned some money.' She sat up, all brisk and businesslike. 'I think I'll get going tomorrow. So, Rosa, you had better come to say goodbye to me before you go to school in the morning as I shan't be here when you get back.'

Now, I had lined up all sorts of questions about

the book, such as 'What does "base libel" mean, and "valuation" and "assessors"?' There were loads of tricky words like these in *The Wind in the Willows*, and I had found that when I asked about them I was always taken seriously, unlike my requests for glasses of water. I could squeeze a good few extra minutes before lights out if I played my cards right and asked the right sort of questions.

However, her startling announcement drove all other thoughts from my head. I had got used to her being around. I liked the smell of her and I liked our trips out and about. I sat bolt upright in bed and looked first to Auntie Maggie for confirmation. She gave me a sad little smile and a small nod. I checked Uncle Bert, who looked solemn. Then I flung my arms around the Perfumed Lady's neck and asked in a small voice if she really had to go. Couldn't she stay with us and work in the cafe, I asked.

Of course, I had already realized that this was not an option because it was obvious that the grown-ups had already discussed things and the decision had been made. To be absolutely truthful, I couldn't imagine her behind the counter, up to her elbows in greasy washing-up water, or getting up early enough in the morning to serve the breakfasts. But it was worth a try. I was going to miss her.

She gave me a hug and kissed the top of my head, then disentangled herself from my skinny arms and left the room in a hurry.

Auntie Maggie heaved herself to her feet and came over to me. She cuddled and stroked me, and murmured that I wasn't to worry, that I'd see my mum again, that she would still take me places, that it had all been settled, that she would come to visit often. Eventually, I allowed myself to be comforted enough to feel sleepy and I was tucked up and kissed goodnight. Auntie Maggie and Uncle Bert filed out of my room, closing the door quietly behind them.

The next morning, I went into her room to say goodbye but she was still dozy. She managed a drowsy 'Cheerio. See you soon. Be a good girl,' and then I had to go to school. Sure enough, she'd packed and left by the time I got home. The only evidence that she had ever been there was a waste-paper basket full of bits of make-up-smeared cotton wool, a half-full bottle of flame-red nail polish called 'Jezebel', some magazines and my precious store of books.

The Perfumed Lady left on that Monday and it

wasn't long before our life at the cafe returned to its well-ordered pattern. I'm ashamed to say that for all my fuss of the night before, the familiar routine closed over the gap that she left in no time at all and you couldn't even see the seam. Auntie Maggie and Uncle Bert would keep the customers well supplied with grub, beverages and gossip. Madame Zelda, Paulette and Luigi were in every day, usually several times, and were my favourite regulars. Sharky came in when he decided he needed solid refreshment for a change, or some information as to the whereabouts of 'esteemed clients' of the more slippery kind. Ronnie from the market had his dinner with us on weekdays, while someone minded his stall. Auntie Maggie used to tease him, saying we paid good money for his veg and then the bleeder came and ate it all. He would counter by telling her that this hardly mattered as he was still paying through the nose for it, wasn't he?

School was OK too. Kathy and I had become quite friendly after our fight and a small group of us hung around together. Lessons had taken on a new interest because we were rapidly approaching the Coronation. We were busy boning up on all things to do with our monarchy. The bits about the crown and the crown jewels were fun, and we heard about Elizabeth I, how we were the 'New Elizabethans' and how we were about to enter a 'Golden Age'. Elizabeth II's lineage was explored and we discovered how she came to be Queen. The abdication of her uncle, Edward VIII, was skipped over pretty quickly and our teacher, Miss Small, tried to move hastily on to the reign of Elizabeth's father. The story of Edward VIII's affair with a married woman, who, what's more, had been divorced, was not considered suitable for our young ears but of course I didn't realize this and began to wave my hand about. I had information and was determined to pass it on. I'd heard the grown-ups at home talking about it and there was no holding me.

'Yes, Rosa, what is it?'

'It's Edward VIII, miss. He was having it off with that Simpson woman, my auntie Maggie said so. Terrible it was. She was a divorced woman, miss, *and* still married to Mr Simpson. He was her second husband, I think, or maybe her third. Anyway, she'd had more than her share, my auntie Maggie says. She was still married to this Simpson bloke when she got off with the King, miss, only he was the Prince of Wales then of course. Madame Zelda says that the Queen's mum never really forgave them for landing her old man in it and him with that awful stutter too, miss, that's what she says.'

I was just about to launch into how they'd been sent to live abroad and were not allowed back in England when Miss Small managed to attract my attention.

'I'm sure that is all very interesting, Rosa, although your turn of phrase could do with a little work, I feel. Let us move away from Edward VIII and get back to the Queen's father, shall we?'

'Oh, miss,' my classmates, who loved a good scandal, wailed in disappointment. What Miss Small failed to understand, coming from Hampshire as she did, was that it took more than illicit sex and divorce to shock Soho children or even to surprise them. Let's face it, it was the stuff of our everyday life. Some of our mothers sold sex for a living and others had a lively trade in being professional co-respondents. One or two of us even had divorced parents. So stories of such things concerning royalty only made them more human to us.

So, with all these distractions, I barely missed my mum after the first day or so. It was probably just as well. I think I'd already realized that she was not someone you could rely on, otherwise I wouldn't have been so frightened at the thought that she could take me away. Don't get me wrong, I liked her all right. It was just that I'd cottoned on that she couldn't stand the weight of being needed. She had to travel light.

8

It wasn't long after the Perfumed Lady left that the stranger showed up at the cafe for the first time. He bought cups of tea and sat in the corner by the window, managing to drag each cuppa out for ages, according to Auntie Maggie. He just sat smoking, drinking his tea and watching the street. It was almost dinner time before he finally left. Next day he was back, and the day after and the one after that. Then he disappeared as mysteriously as he had come. His routine over those few days had never varied: cups of tea, a window seat and lots of fags. Auntie Maggie began to suspect that he was watching and waiting for someone but whoever it was never showed up.

He reappeared a month later. I know it was about a month because they had let me have the day off school on account of the Queen's Coronation the next day, Tuesday. So I saw him. He was a pretty ordinary-looking bloke except for his eyes, which were never still. The really weird thing about them, though, was that one was blue and the other was brown. Of course this fascinated me and I kept finding excuses to lurk around him so that I could get a better look. I think he cottoned on because in the end he hissed out of the side of his mouth for me to 'bugger off'. There was something sinister about that hiss, so off I buggered, toot sweet, I can tell you. I scampered over to help Auntie Maggie, and didn't mention the hissing because I was pretty sure she'd tell me it served me right for staring.

We were closing a bit early that day; a rare event, but it wasn't every day that a queen got crowned, was it? We had to prepare for the great day. The actual crowning was to take place in the morning, which meant that our Coronation knees-up would last all day and most of the night. Everyone we knew was invited to the party.

You can imagine the rush and bustle about the place. Between customers, Auntie Maggie, Uncle Bert and I were busy trying to decorate the cafe. We were aiming for a patriotic look so there was red, white and blue everywhere. There wasn't a spider plant, geranium or wandering Jew in the place that didn't have its little Union Jack on a stick poking out of it. A small forest of the things was stuck in the top of the tea urn, but the steam was making them hang limp like damp washing. I thought they looked miserable and disheartened, rather than proud and jaunty like they were supposed to look. Red, white and blue streamers hung from the ceiling and the light fittings, forcing everyone to dodge and weave so that the ends didn't flap into their bacon and eggs or cups of tea.

Any surface that didn't have a punter sitting at it had plates waiting to be piled high with biscuits, fancy little cakes and sandwiches. While they waited, they were being elaborately decorated with frilly doilies and miniature Union Jacks. Some things were still rationed and there were lots of shortages but somehow this never seemed to cramp Uncle Bert's and Auntie Maggie's style one little bit. Of course, we did live in a place where wheeling and dealing were second nature to virtually anyone or anything with a heartbeat, and our cafe always seemed to have things like sugar, cheese and meat even when rationing was at its meanest. A constant stream of men with patent-leather hair and sharp suits saw that we were kept well stocked. They'd sidle in the kitchen door, eyes darting this way and that, just like the hissing mystery man's, as they displayed their wares from battered suitcases. In their time they had sold everything from sugar, butter, eggs and corned beef to stockings and dresses. Uncle Bert and Auntie Maggie always got a good deal because they had what the local villains always referred to as 'respect'.

Anyway, there we were, trying to feed and water the customers and prepare for the party all at the same time. The sleazy article with the odd, shifty eyes was still stuck in the window, slurping tea, smoking and watching the street like a hawk. He was checking out the passers-by with his busy eyes and I was watching him because he made me nervous. I had my beady eye on him when he stiffened as if he'd seen a ghost and then ducked hastily so that his head was almost under the table. I tried to work out who or what he had seen but it wasn't until the cafe door opened that I realized that the object of his attention was Madame Zelda. She breezed in, oblivious to the panic she'd caused, and started to chat with Auntie Maggie. Once she had her back to him, he got up and headed stealthily towards the door. I'm not sure why I did it, perhaps it was because he'd hissed at me or maybe I just thought that Madame Zelda ought to know he was there.

'Auntie Maggie,' I piped up in clear, ringing tones. 'Did that bloke that's leaving pay for his teas?'

He froze with his hand on the doorknob, the babble of voices suddenly died and Auntie Maggie's eyes narrowed as she glared at the retreating back.

'Just a minute, mate. Haven't you forgotten something? Rosie's right, you haven't coughed up for your teas. That'll be sixpence, if you please.'

Madame Zelda turned to look and all the colour drained from her face. Her mouth opened and closed like a fish out of water but it took a moment for her voice to co-operate.

'Charlie Fluck! What the bleedin' hell are you doing here?'

Just for a second, he looked as if he was about to bolt, then he straightened and turned. 'I could arst you the same thing, Enie. What the bleedin' hell are *you* doing here?'

They stared at each other across the room like a pair of dogs who were trying to work out whether to go for the throat. You could have heard a pin drop as we waited for the drama to unfold. Then Uncle Bert appeared in the kitchen doorway, wiping his hands on a towel. He took in the scene at a glance.

'Have we got some kind of problem here?' he asked quietly. 'What's the matter, mate? Can't you pay or what? We ain't running a charity, you know.'

Charlie Fluck began to bluster. 'Hang on a minute. It was merely some kind of hoversight. Course I was going . . .'

Uncle Bert held up a hand. 'Just cough up what you owe, there's a good lad. Then we can all get on.' He turned to Madame Zelda. 'Do you know this bloke, Zelda?'

Madame Zelda nodded, her eyes bright with anger. 'I asked you what you was doing here, Charlie, and I want an answer. If you've come looking for me, you can just bugger off again. You and me was finished years ago and bloody glad I was too. Now, what the hell do you want? Spit it out, then crawl back under your stone where you belong.'

Charlie was on his dignity. 'If you think I'm going to discuss my private business in front of these nosy buggers, you are very much mistaken, my gel.'

Madame Zelda's face turned an interesting shade of purple. 'Don't you "my gel" me, you low-life,' she exploded. Madame Zelda was never one to tart it up, and still isn't, come to that. 'I said spit it out. There ain't nothing you can say to me that I don't want these people to hear. They're my friends and a million times more use to me than you ever was, you toe-rag.'

While this was going on, every eye and ear in the place was hanging on each word and gesture, heads were turning from Madame Zelda to Charlie Fluck as if watching a ping-pong match and we were all very glad that Madame Zelda didn't seem to need privacy.

Uncle Bert, however, had other ideas. 'That's it, folks. Show's over. It's time we closed for the day anyway. We've got a knees-up to organize. Come on now, give us a chance. Eat and drink up. It's time to go.'

There was some disgruntled muttering but the punters began to trickle out of the door.

'Zelda, am I right in thinking that you do know this bloke? And am I also right in thinking that you wish you didn't?' Uncle Bert continued. 'If you want to talk to him here where you've got friends to make sure he doesn't get up to anything, you're very welcome. The corner table is your best bet. Maggie, get her a cuppa. She looks as if she could do with one. Rosie, you carry on helping your auntie Maggie. Yell if you need me.'

Madame Zelda and Charlie Fluck settled down at

the corner table and I was put to work by my aunt. It was really hard to overhear what was going on between the two of them and believe me I tried. I kept drifting over towards their table and every time she noticed, Auntie Maggie would grab some part of my anatomy and steer me away. It became quite a game and she and I were red in the face with repressed giggles by the time Madame Zelda exploded in another rage.

'Now listen here, Charlie Fluck, you was a bastard when we was married and I see no reason to believe that you've changed one little bit. I 'aven't wasted my time even thinking about you since you buggered off and left me for that tart of a cousin of mine. I'm glad to see she's had the sense to get rid of you at last. I've made a life for meself and you, you great pillock, are *not* going to muscle in on it. Get that into your thick head once and for all.'

I couldn't hear what Charlie had to say about this outburst because he never raised his voice above a wheedling whine, but whatever it was failed to impress our Madame Zelda. She leaped to her feet and fetched him an almighty clout around the ear with her handbag. This might not sound much, but if you take into account that her handbag invariably contained a small, portable crystal ball, a well-thumbed pack of tarot cards and about half a ton of black market sweets as well as the usual stuff, you'll get the picture. The blow stopped him mid-wheedle and he slid, in slow motion, down his chair and ended up in an unconscious heap on the floor.

The commotion attracted the attention of my aunt and uncle and Mrs Wong, who had come in to help prepare for the party. They gathered around Charlie's crumpled form and stared down at him with a variety of expressions.

Auntie Maggie looked deeply satisfied. She and Madame Zelda were good friends and she undoubtedly knew a fair bit about Charlie Fluck and, judging by her expression, what she knew she didn't like. Her look suggested that Charlie was something that had come in on someone's shoe and that it was high time he was cleared up. Uncle Bert, on the other hand, looked like a refuse collector, sizing up the difficulties of getting shot of this unwanted heap. Mrs Wong's expression was, as ever, inscrutable, although there was perhaps just a hint of a smile. Madame Zelda had a look that was a mixture of triumph and astonishment. Me, I danced around whooping like a Red Indian, I'm not sure why, but I'd taken against Charlie Fluck and I was overexcited by the prospect of the coming party. Nobody seemed to mind my unholy glee, however. As one, they turned their backs on the bundle and settled down at another table.

As Madame Zelda began to explain about Charlie, I kept as quiet and as unobtrusive as possible. I was mortally afraid that someone would notice me and decide that this subject was not suitable for a mere child. It's galling just how often adults decide what you can and cannot hear.

It turned out that Madame Zelda and Charlie Fluck had been brought up near each other in somewhere called Dalston Junction. Later I learned that this was in the East End. It's not really important to know that, but I just like to know the ins and outs of a louse's lug'ole according to Uncle Bert. Anyway, they had started going out together when they were very young. Poor Madame Zelda was just seventeen when 'that bastard Charlie' got her 'in the family way'. I was dying to know what 'family way' meant, but I didn't dare ask because I was pretty sure I'd be banished upstairs if they remembered I was there. They had a hasty 'shotgun' wedding and settled down in two rooms in Mare Street. About a month after the wedding, Charlie got legless one night and in a rage threw Madame Zelda down the stairs and kicked her over and over again as she lay helpless. She ended up in hospital and lost her baby. She said she'd never forgiven him for it. With tears welling up in her eyes she explained that she'd tried for a baby several more times after that, but had never been able to hang on to one. It was at this point in the story that Auntie Maggie noticed me sitting there with my mouth wide open. I had never seen Madame Zelda so upset before.

'Hang on a minute, Zeld, there's a couple of little harkers flapping away here that shouldn't be. Rosie, you go upstairs now and tidy your bedroom, there's a good girl. It's a tip.'

I knew there was no point in arguing, but I tried pleading anyway, just in case it worked. It didn't. I was sent, dragging my heels, to sort out my room. Naturally I didn't really go. I thumped my way up the stairs, making as much row as possible, partly as a protest and partly so that they would all be sure I'd gone. Then I slipped my shoes off and padded silently back down again and lurked just behind the door, which I had thoughtfully left open a crack. I had eavesdropping down to a fine art; I expect most kids do who live in an entirely adult set-up. It's hard to be left out when you're the only child in the place. Of course, if you have hordes of brothers and sisters, I expect you're too busy playing and squabbling to take much notice of grown-up affairs.

I had just got settled comfortably behind the door and was trying to breathe quietly when I heard a soft groaning sound. I was wondering what on earth it could be when Uncle Bert kindly told me.

'The little bastard's coming round. Do you want me to put him out again for you, Zelda? Or would you rather do it yourself?'

There was a pause, presumably so that Madame Zelda could weigh up her options. 'No, it's all right, ta. There's Luigi and a few of his mates. We could ask them to dump him somewhere out of the way.'

I heard someone rapping on the window and the cafe door being unbolted and then Luigi's voice. 'Watcha, all. What can I do for you?'

'Could you get rid of that somewhere for me, Luigi? I want shot of the bleeder.'

Luigi sounded embarrassed. 'I dunno, Madame Zelda. Snuffing's not really in my line. You'd be better off with Sid the Shiv or maybe Mad Albie'll do it for you. He likes that kinda thing. Course, he'll have to check it out with Maltese Joe first. He may not like Albie freelancing. Who is he and what's he done, anyway?'

'Don't be daft, Luigi. I ain't asking you to bump the bugger off. I just want him removed from the premises and dumped on a bomb site or somewhere until he comes round and crawls back to the sewer he came out of. He's my husband, if you must know. He just turned up looking for someone and came across me by mistake. I'll tell you more about it when he's gone. He may look out for the count but you can bet your life he's earwigging even as we speak.'

I heard a gusty sigh of relief and Luigi's voice drifted through the crack in the door. 'Oh, is that all? Yeah, we can get rid of him for you. How far away do you want him? Oy, you lot. Get in here and scrape him up, will you? We're taking him on a little trip. South London do you, Madame Zelda? We were heading that way anyway. We've heard there's a big game on down Clapham way. We thought we'd relieve 'em of a few bob, didn't we, lads?'

There was a murmur of agreement and negotiations continued in tones too low for me to hear. Eventually I heard the cafe door open and close again.

Auntie Maggie's voice boomed in the silence that followed their departure. 'Well, that's got shot of him. You can tell us now – what was he doing here anyway? If he wasn't looking for you, who was he looking for? He was definitely keeping his eyes peeled for someone, that's for sure.'

'Well, that's it, see. I'm not sure. He said he was looking for a woman called Cassandra Loveday-Smythe. I told him I'd never heard of her. Then I remembered that our Rosie's mum is called Cassandra something or other and wondered if it might be her. Course, I never let on. I just asked him why he was so keen to find her. He tapped his nose and said that that would be telling. You can bet your life the slimy little git is up to no bleeding good. He says he works for her dad as a chauffeur, and learned to drive in the war. Do you think he's talking about Rosie's mum?'

Uncle Bert sounded alarmed. 'Did 'e tell you anything else? Any details that might give us a clue? Cassie's name is Smith as far as I know, but I never was convinced by it. Course, some poor sods have got to be called Smith and I don't s'pose anyone ever believes 'em. If she wanted to disappear, changing her name would be her first move. Mind you, it's a bit close to Smythe for comfort, but amateurs always do that, pick a name close to their own. I s'pose it's comforting.'

The talk continued but I hardly heard it. I was trying to take it all in. Any information about my mum was news to me and it always made my stomach tighten and my heart lurch. She made me nervous, my mum did.

I came to just in time to hear Auntie Maggie's tread and voice approaching my hideout. I barely made it up the stairs. I couldn't pretend I'd been tidying my room because it was still a tip so I launched myself at my bed and grabbed a book. It was only after she'd poked her head round the door and tutted at me for being 'a lazy little tyke' that I realized I had it upside down.

9

The next day was Coronation Day!

I was beside myself with excitement for all sorts of reasons. Probably the most thrilling was the fact that Uncle Bert had invested in a television set. He had bought it specially to watch the Queen being crowned, which just goes to show what a big deal it all was. At school my chest had swelled with pride the day after he brought it home. They were thin on the ground in those days, tellies were, and I was the first of my schoolmates to have one. Being the natural swanker that I was, and probably still am, I got plenty of mileage out of it. Auntie Maggie told me that I could invite my friends round to watch it if I liked. Did I like? Not being one to let an opportunity slip past me, of course I did! It was quickly agreed that a few of my friends could stay and party until the grown-ups really got going, then perhaps it would be better if they buggered off home.

I was also dying to see the crown, the Queen's dress and all the jewels. Me, Patsy, Jill, Jenny and Kathy Moon had, of course, been playing coronations for weeks with an old velvet curtain for a train and a cardboard crown. Paulette had given me all sorts of bits and pieces like paste diamonds and sequins to decorate it. The whole effect was splendid. That cardboard crown twinkled and shone almost as well as the real thing. For an orb we had a rubber ball covered in silver paper and more of Paulette's gems. I can't remember what our sceptre was made of – cardboard, I suppose. We thought we looked wonderful as we took it in turns to strut about being the Queen. I expect you're wondering what that cow Kathy Moon was doing joining in the proceedings. It's just amazing what making somebody's nose bleed can do.

When I finally got to see the real Coronation the bit that deeply impressed me was the coach and horses. We still saw the odd horse here and there delivering things but these were different. Much smarter they were, all done up in fancy gear and everything matching. They were beautiful. I tried for days after to get Tom to act as a horse, but he wasn't having any. He just hissed and scratched and by the time I gave it up I looked as if I'd been savaged by a demented hedgehog.

Of course, the other great excitement besides showing off the television set and finally getting to see the event that had been heralded for so many months was the party. Auntie Maggie and Uncle Bert really knew how to throw a bash and all my favourite people were there. I tended to get spoilt rotten by all and sundry and of course I lapped it up.

It seems to me that people in those days had the corner on having a good time. Life had been grim. Austerity was a word much bandied about, and it said it all. There had been years and years of fear, death, injury, separation, rationing and endless shortages for most people. Everywhere you looked there were reminders. Bomb sites gaped like broken teeth, pathetic reminders of just how temporary life could be.

Uncle Bert seemed preoccupied as the finishing touches were being put to the food and decorations. He kept going next door to Sharky's to use the telephone, but whoever he was trying to reach was out. Whenever this happened he'd go into a huddle with Auntie Maggie and look worried. Every now and then he'd take a look out of the window and each time he did so, his expression got grimmer.

This went on for a bit and then he seemed to come to some kind of decision. He grabbed me by the scruff of the neck as I hurried past with a trayful of meat paste sandwiches and told me to nip up the road and get Luigi. I was on the point of making the ritual protest, the sort that comes out as a sort of wail and usually starts with a long-drawn-out '*Ohhh*', and had my gob open to begin when I caught the look in his eye and snapped it shut. I nipped, and with alacrity. On the way, I caught a glimpse of Madame Zelda's Charlie lurking in a doorway, eyes peeled. I figured that Uncle Bert's uneasiness had something to do with him and hurried along faster.

The Campaninis' delicatessen had, and still has, the most tantalizing smell. It's a combination of fresh coffee, herbs, garlic, spicy sausages and musty dried mushrooms all piled on top of the sweet scent of vanilla and something else I can't quite identify, chocolate maybe. It is so good it's tempting to grab a spoon and try to eat it.

The back of the shop was dedicated to the selling of groceries. Shelves were stacked up the walls and groaned under the weight of packets, tins and jars filled with mysterious goodies. As England squirmed out from the grip of rationing, so the cabinets began to fill slowly with cheeses, cold meats, dishes of olives and delicious concoctions that swam in olive oil and tomato sauce. Fresh ravioli, tortellini and spaghetti were also available. Various Campanini daughters and wives were pressed into service producing the stuff. Ravioli was popular in hard times, as all sorts could be ground up and stuffed into it and no one was any the wiser. It also made a very little meat go a very long way.

Huddled in a corner towards the front of the shop were a few tables opposite a gleaming counter dominated by a hissing coffee machine. Bolted firmly to one end of the counter was a heavy green metal contraption which had a jaunty red trim, a large wheel with a brass handle and a big funnel on top. The funnel was attached to a bulbous body that housed a grinding mechanism and there was a sliding drawer below. This was the coffee grinder, idle during the war, but coming back to life now that some precious beans were filtering through from South America. Soldiers home on leave flocked to Mamma Campanini's to buy packets of fresh coffee beans to take back to Germany with them where they could be flogged for a month's wages.

The beans were stored in large black and gold tins that stood on a sparkling glass and chrome shelf. Exotic names like Costa Rica, Brazil and Continental Roast were emblazoned on their fronts. I asked Auntie Maggie what all the names meant and she told me they were places, so I fetched an atlas and spent a few happy hours trying to track them all down. I couldn't understand what had happened to Continental Roast though I did find Continental Shelf, but that seemed to be in the sea. It was ages before I found out that Continental Roast was a description and not a place.

A lot of shops hadn't troubled to open on Coronation Day but Mamma Campanini was behind her grocery counter as usual when I flew through the door. Not that she wasn't patriotic, it was just that she was coming to our place later on and had nothing much to do before she came. The younger Campanini women were seeing to the grub that was their contribution to our party, so Mamma opened the store for a couple of hours for the benefit of the disorganized who needed last-minute supplies before the royal kick-off at about half past ten.

Mamma's face split into a huge grin at the sight of me hurtling through her door, puffing and panting and full of self-importance. Her two gold teeth flashed and gleamed among the regulation white ones. I loved those gold teeth and thought they added a note of distinction.

I was definitely one of Mamma's favourites. It was the blond curls, blue eyes and my passing resemblance to a certain princess that did it. Under normal circumstances I would have been offered a huge bowl of cassata ice cream as soon as I appeared. However, there must have been a sense of urgency about me because there was no such offer that day, much to my disappointment. I especially liked the glacé fruit, the nuts, and the green bits which were my favourite.

Mamma's grin turned to a look of enquiry as I blurted out Uncle Bert's request for Luigi. She trundled over to the door at the back and roared up the stairs. 'Luigi, getta down 'ere. You have a younga lady a waiting for you.'

There was a muffled reply and she bade me wait a minute. He'd be down, she told me, and slipped me a handful of almonds coated in a sugary sort of stuff to munch while I waited. Mamma Campanini could not bear the thought of anyone being peckish, however briefly. I chewed and shuffled from foot to foot as she continued to serve her customers.

Eventually I heard footsteps on the stairs and the door opened and there was Luigi, comb in hand. As usual, I noticed his large brown eyes, sparkling with the joys of life, and realized perhaps for the first time that he really was tall, dark and handsome. He gave his mother a resounding but affectionate whack on the backside as he passed her and came round the front of the counter. She giggled, and thumped his shoulder playfully.

'Yes, Shorty, what can I do for you?'

'Uncle Bert says can you come? It's important.'

'OK, I'm on me way.' He turned to his mother. 'Tell Alberto where I am if he asks for me. Ciao, Mamma.'

The street was getting even busier as we made our way to the cafe. There was a feeling of anticipation in the air and people were bustling to get things done so that they could go home and huddle around tellies and wirelesses with family and friends. Everyone knew that they were about to witness a piece of history that had nothing to do with bombs, mutilated bodies or shattered lives. It made a wonderful change. The Coronation was a hopeful thing and reinforced the feeling that British was best. Not that anyone had any real doubts. We'd won the war, hadn't we? We had the Empire. Of course

British was best, but the Coronation rubber-stamped it somehow.

Luigi heaved me on to his shoulders for the short trip from the deli to the cafe. We arrived with me giggling fit to bust and we had to duck to get me safely through the door. I was so thrilled with my ride that I completely forgot to look out for Charlie on the way back.

Once I had been delivered to ground level again, it was all business. Uncle Bert didn't beat about the bush.

'I'm glad you could come, Luigi. Madame Zelda's old man has been hanging about all morning. We think he's looking for Rosie's mum, but we don't know why. One thing Madame Zelda is sure of, though, is that the little bastard's up to no good. Whatever he wants our Cassie for, you can bet your life it won't be to her advantage. Madame Zelda told him yesterday that she'd never heard of this Cassandra person, but he obviously really believes she's round here somewhere, otherwise he wouldn't be skulking in doorways. Trouble is, she's due here any time. I've been trying to get her on the blower but I can't get no answer. Have you any idea where she is?'

Luigi shook his head. 'Who knows? You know

what she's like. She's probably holed up in a hotel with some geezer. The place is stiff with tourists here for the Coronation. The clubs was bursting at the seams last night and the girls was so busy they hardly had time to get their drawers back on between punters. Blokes from the sticks think they've died and gone to heaven when they get up to the Smoke and see all them lovely girls.'

Uncle Bert nodded and looked grim. He scratched his head and pondered for a bit. Auntie Maggie bustled past with a huge plate of fairy cakes and dumped them on one of the tables, then joined the two men in their discussions. Luigi offered to go hunting for the Perfumed Lady but Auntie Maggie was practical.

'Don't be daft. Where would you start? You said the place was heaving. Anyway, there's no time. Even with a motor you'd be hard pressed. The streets are already choked with people. They said on the wireless no one could remember ever seeing such a mob. No, we'd be better off doing something about him rather than looking for her.'

Both men looked at her with admiration. It was so simple when you thought about it. Uncle Bert slipped his arm around her huge waist and gave her a squeeze. Auntie Maggie blushed and leaned into him a bit, looking pleased.

'Good thinking, Maggie my love. You ain't just a pretty face. You got brains an' all. Of course that's the answer. Now, any suggestions as to what we can do with him?'

I still hadn't entirely recovered from being hissed at, so I shoved in my two penn'orth at that point. I remembered the bunches of sausages and salami at the deli and danced around the little group. 'We could chop him up and turn him into salami,' I suggested helpfully.

Three pairs of eyes turned on me with a faint air of astonishment. Only Uncle Bert joined in the spirit of the thing. 'A good idea, Rosie, but the bleeder's too scrawny. He'd never make a decent sausage, not enough meat on him. Suppose we clobber him and shove him in the cellar for the duration? We could always leave him something to eat and drink.'

Auntie Maggie was not keen. 'Say he has to go to the toilet? I don't want to have to clean up after him. Anyway, he'd make a row, yelling and that. We don't want him spoiling the Coronation for us, do we? Old Bill might not understand, either. You never know, the slimy little git might make a complaint. Even with your connections, Bert, it'd take some getting out of. Ain't that kidnap or something? Could cost a fair old bit in back'anders, kidnapping could.'

There was silence as everyone considered the implications. Then Auntie Maggie roared, 'I've got it! Couldn't we send him on a wild-goose chase? Somewhere a nice long way away.'

Once again the men eyed her with unconcealed admiration. 'Make it far enough and we could be shot of the little sod all day,' she continued. 'It'd give us time to warn our Cassie if she shows up here.'

A lively discussion followed. It was decided that Luigi should do the honours by offering to sell the information as to Cassie's whereabouts to Charlie. The general opinion was that Charlie was so bent, he'd never believe in a freebie. The stumbling block was how to explain away Luigi's knowledge of Charlie's quest to find my mum. He hadn't been there when Madame Zelda told us about it and Charlie knew it.

Madame Zelda provided the answer in person when she rapped imperiously on the cafe door.

Auntie Maggie let her in. 'Watcha, Zeld. Have you seen your Charlie this morning? He's been hanging about since first thing. We've just been discussing how to get shot of him. We don't want Cassie showing up here while he's on the lookout. We've tried warning her by blower but there's no answer.'

Madame Zelda was indignant. 'Don't call him "my Charlie". He ain't been mine for years now, I'm pleased to say.'

'We decided that Luigi here should tip him the wink that Cassie's in Brighton or somewhere with a rich punter, but we can't decide how Luigi's supposed to have found out that Charlie's looking for her,' Uncle Bert told her.

Madame Zelda came up with the solution in a flash. 'That's easy. If Charlie's watching, then he saw Luigi come in and now he's seen me. I could be telling you all about it. When Luigi heads for home, he could spot the toe-rag, lure him to a quiet spot and flog him the news.'

In less than an hour, Luigi was back, mission accomplished. Charlie was happily on his way to Brighton, Luigi was a few quid richer and Madame Zelda was cackling like a regular army of hens. She liked the idea of getting one over on Charlie – she liked it a lot.

10

The Coronation was lovely even though the weather was lousy. Some said that it was the coldest June day they could ever remember, and that the poor sods sleeping on the pavement the night before certainly earned their glimpse of the Queen.

My mates were suitably impressed by our telly. We sat close up, noses almost mashed against the screen. The grown-ups had to keep telling us to sit back a bit, that *they* couldn't see. We scrutinized every last detail of the Queen's frock, crown, coach and all. We got fits of giggles during the procession out of the abbey when they started to talk about 'Mistresses of the Robes'. 'Ladies and Women of the Bedchamber' had us in hysterics and not one of the adults could tell us why some were 'ladies' and others were just 'women'. Still, Auntie Maggie,

Madame Zelda and Paulette had a fine old time speculating about what these females got up to in the Queen's bedroom and if there was any room for her old man with that lot cluttering up the place. Mamma Campanini and old Mrs Roberts contented themselves with pretending to be shocked, pursing their lips and shaking their heads between outbursts of merriment.

Food and drink flowed freely and there was a general air of rejoicing. The Perfumed Lady, my mum, managed to miss the ceremony altogether of course. She rolled in an hour or two after, when the party was in full swing. She had a bloke in tow and they were both lit up like the Blackpool illuminations, having been on the razzle all night. Auntie Maggie and Uncle Bert tried to tell her about Charlie, but it was a pointless exercise as she was in no condition to take it in. I was charged with keeping an eye on her, and if she tried to leave I had to tip Uncle Bert, Auntie Maggie or Madame Zelda the wink. They had decided that the best thing to do was to hang on to her until she sobered up a bit. Then they could explain about Charlie and all.

My friends went home once the new Queen was safely back at her gaff. We'd watched the great occasion, eaten and drunk until we felt sick and were well satisfied. There was a sort of a break after my mates left when people drifted in and out and it all went a bit quiet. Auntie Maggie put me to bed for a nap, promising that I could join the party later when things got going again. I slept like the dead.

It was getting dark by the time I came to again. I could hear music and the rise and fall of voices. There was smoke in the air, cigars, cigarettes and Uncle Bert's pipe. Every now and then there was a thumping noise as people stumped up the stairs to go to the toilet. The piano that usually stood in the corner of the cafe under an old flowered curtain was tinkling away. It sounded like a good party with the hum of conversation competing with the sounds of singing and dancing. I sat up, put my bedside light on – and there on a chair was a dress I had never seen before.

It was really beautiful, just like the ones the Italian girls wore at Christmas and on saints' days. It was dark blue satin, all shiny with delicate bits of creamy lace around the collar. It had a waistband that could be tied at the back in a huge bow and short, puffed sleeves, and a neat row of tiny pearl buttons down the front of the bodice gleamed against the dark satin, the skirt was full and there was a petticoat to put underneath it. This was almost better than the dress. It was made of layers and layers of stiff net, with frothy lace at the bottom that matched the lace on the collar of the frock. Once the whole thing was on, the skirt of the dress stood out proud with a hint of lace peeping out from below the hem. Beneath the chair, a pair of black patent-leather shoes with a crossbar and tiny holes set in a pattern of flowers stood neatly side by side. God knows where Auntie Maggie got such a gorgeous outfit. Fancy gear was still difficult to find and clothes still tended to be practical and rather sombre. I leaped out of bed and was about to dive into my new stuff when I remembered my training, and slid into the bathroom for a wash first.

I got dressed very carefully and even dragged a brush through my curls. At last I was ready except for tying my bow at the back. I couldn't manage that by myself. I was only just getting the hang of bows and then only frontwise. I gave it up in the end and left it as a loose knot. I could always get some friendly grown-up to do the honours before I made my entrance downstairs. A fairly constant stream of possible volunteers were coming up and down stairs to use the facilities.

Before joining the party, I crept along the passage to Auntie Maggie's and Uncle Bert's room as I wanted to have a dekko at myself in the long mirror on their wardrobe. I sidled in and had just turned round to face the room when I realized that I was not alone. Madame Zelda was standing by the edge of the big bed cradling something and rocking gently back and forth. She was murmuring softly, almost crooning, the way you do with babies and I had to strain to hear, her voice was so quiet.

'There, there, love. Don't carry on so. The little shit was never worth it, you know that. Be honest with youself, petal. He was never worth it. Better you should find out now than carry on keeping the bastard. There now, you have a good cry. It'll do you good.'

There was the sound of muffled sobs and choking hiccups coming from somewhere in the region of Madame Zelda's bosom. I was just about to beat a hasty retreat – you get a sixth sense about these things when you're the only kid in the place – when Madame Zelda caught sight of me. She straightened and gave the hiccuping figure a gentle pat on the back.

'Well, look what we've got here, Paulette love. Doesn't she look a picture? You stay put, Rosie, and show Paulette your nice new frock. You look lovely, dear, you really do. Take a gander at her quick, Paulette.'

The heaving shoulders began to subside and after much snivelling Paulette straightened and wiped her nose on the back of her hand. She turned round and gave me a watery smile. Her hair was all over the place and her nose was red and oozing. Black mascara tracks meandered down her puffy cheeks.

'Ooh, Rosie, that blue suits you, it really does. Shows up your eyes something wonderful.' Paulette's chin trembled but she took a deep, wrenching breath and smiled at me as the tears ran steadily down her grubby face.

I am an old hand at grubby faces and tears and knew exactly what to do. Luckily, the bathroom was empty and I was back in a trice with a wet flannel and a dry towel. Silently, I handed them to Madame Zelda who began tenderly to wash and wipe Paulette's face. I went to Uncle Bert's drawer and came back with a clean neatly ironed and folded handkerchief and handed it to Paulette. She took it absent-mindedly, then crumpled it into her fist and stuffed it into her mouth as another wrenching sob rose up in her.

'Blow hard, Paulette, that's what Auntie Maggie always says,' I told her. 'It helps clear your head and things look a bit better when your head's clear.'

Paulette made a valiant attempt at a laugh. It

wobbled a bit, then, suddenly, she was all business. She sat up straight, struggled free of Madame Zelda's comforting arms, took the flannel off her and gave her own face a thorough wipe round. Next she dried it on the white towel and gave her nose a gigantic blow into Uncle Bert's Christmas hanky. She stood up, smoothed her skirt down her thighs and fumbled in her cheap white plastic clutch bag for a compact and a comb. She gazed long and hard into the little round mirror, sniffed and then began to dab her shiny red nose with the powder puff. Finally she pulled the comb through her tangled hair and applied a liberal coating of lipstick. Compact, comb, lipstick and hanky were stuffed back into her bag. She tucked her chin in, straightened her shoulders and smiled wanly at Madame Zelda and me.

'Right,' she said. 'Time to show those bastards what's what. Come here, Rosie love, and I'll tie your bow.'

'That's my girl, you shove yer best foot forward,' Madame Zelda encouraged. 'No point in shedding any more tears over that slimy little git. I always thought 'e came in on yer shoe anyway. Let's escort this little gel in her nice new frock down to the party. Then we can bask in a bit of her glory.'

I led the way down the steep stairs to the cafe

where the party was in full swing. I located Auntie Maggie and Uncle Bert straight away. Auntie Maggie was doing a soft-shoe shuffle with Papa Campanini and Uncle Bert was doling out a drink to Sharky Finn at the counter. Reassured, I took in some of the rest of the action. Luigi was dancing with Gina, one of his many sisters, and Mamma Campanini watched her husband and children from the sidelines, gold teeth glinting in the yellow lamplight as she smiled indulgently.

There were small groups of people scattered about in corners and at tables, chatting, drinking and watching the dancers. Old Mrs Roberts from the paper shop was playing the piano and had been for some time, judging by the number of empty stout bottles that littered its battered top.

From time to time Uncle Bert took over, and so did Madame Zelda. There was never any shortage of pianists at our parties, and they all had their own style. Mrs Roberts was good for all the old tunes like 'Daisy, Daisy' and 'Roll Out the Barrel'. Madame Zelda did comic songs from the music hall, and Uncle Bert did too, only different ones. With all the theatres and clubs around us, there were plenty of volunteers to play the very latest offerings from films, shows and the clubs.

Way over in the corner, I caught sight of Paulette's Dave crawling over some person I had never seen before. He'd brought another girl to our party, knowing full well he was only invited because everyone liked Paulette. No wonder she was fed up – it was humiliating!

Feeling indignant on Paulette's behalf, I turned back to her and took her hand. 'Will you dance with me, Paulette?'

She laughed and said she'd be honoured, and we were off. I danced with everyone that night – Uncle Bert, Auntie Maggie, Luigi, Papa Campanini, Madame Zelda, everyone, except that toe-rag Dave, of course. No one even spoke to him – well, no one who mattered anyhow.

11

The party went on until the early hours of the morning but I missed the last knockings. I was out for the count by midnight; I just couldn't keep my eyes open a second longer, which meant I missed the big fight. I was deeply cheesed off. It was between Dave and T.C. and must have been some barney as everyone was talking about it for days.

It seems that Dave got bored when he realized that Paulette was not going to scratch her rival's eyes out. There had been scenes before and Dave thrived on a bit of conflict as long as it didn't directly include him. In fact there was nothing he liked better than to see two women fighting over him. Anyway, he had laid on a few bets as to who would win his company for the rest of the night and, when there was no fight, he cut his losses by offloading Theresa on some bloke who was willing to pay. Dave was never one to let sentiment get in the way of making a few quid.

Once Theresa had left with her punter, Dave was at a loose end. Paulette wasn't having any when he made a play for her, so he lost his rag and said if she wouldn't come across for him, then she should get her arse out there and hustle. She told him to piss off. She said that she would never work for him again, and that she'd had it – and that was when he hit her. Thrown backwards, she stumbled into T.C.'s missis, Pat, and knocked her clear off her walking sticks.

Well, all hell broke loose! Uncle Bert and Luigi got jammed in the kitchen doorway as they both rushed to help poor Pat up and drag Dave off Paulette. By the time they'd untangled themselves, T.C. had arrived, made sure Pat was all right, settled her in her wheelchair and retrieved her sticks. Then he turned his attention to Dave.

'That's it, out!' T.C.'s crinkly blue eyes no longer had their usual friendly twinkle and he was shaking with rage. Uncle Bert said it was shocking in a funny way, T.C. always being such a mild, even-tempered bloke. I suppose he had to be, being the law and everything.

Dave showed his usual grasp of situations and decided to make something of it.

'Very unwise, that,' Uncle Bert told me the next day. 'Any fool could see that T.C. was not in the mood for any argument. He's very protective of his Pat, is T.C. No one upsets her and gets away with it. Still, if Dave's brains were gunpowder, his hat'd be in no danger.'

I wasn't sure what that meant exactly, but I was pretty sure it wasn't flattering. Heated words were exchanged, but still Dave didn't leave. The next anyone knew, Dave had lost his marbles completely, bared his teeth and took a great lump out of T.C.'s arm. That's when T.C. finally let go of the temper nobody knew he had and proceeded to give Dave what Uncle Bert called 'a very thorough and very satisfying pasting, thank you very much!'

He grabbed Dave around the neck in a headlock and swung him round and round, before suddenly letting him go. Dave staggered into tables and onlookers and finally came to rest against a wall, winded and dizzy. Not one soul made a move to help him. Usually there would have been a stampede to defend one of our own, especially against the burly arm of the law, but as everyone liked T.C. they shoved the loathsome Dave back into the arena and urged the copper to get on with it, whistling and yelling their encouragement.

Only Uncle Bert intervened and that was merely to suggest – or insist – that they carry on in the street to cut down on the damage. It was no contest really. Fry-ups, fags and booze had left Dave a bit flabby when it came to fighting an actual man. Women were more his mark. T.C., on the other hand, was in much better shape and had the benefit of getting plenty of practice in his line of work. Later, everyone said that T.C. could have slaughtered Dave if he'd wanted to and they were a bit disappointed that he hadn't. Dave was bounced off walls and the pavement until he had to beg for mercy, and then T.C. hauled him back into the cafe by the scruff of his neck. Auntie Maggie said by this time he looked just like a rag doll, only bloodier. Dave was dumped on the floor in front of Pat's wheelchair, and T.C.'s toecaps ensured that he grovelled in apology for knocking her over. But this didn't end his humiliation. Once Pat had graciously accepted his apology, he was made to go through the whole thing again with Paulette. Only when he'd done this to everyone's satisfaction did T.C. allow him to stagger off to the Middlesex Hospital to be sewn up. He'd split his lip while cracking his front teeth against T.C.'s boots and eventually had to have them capped, which cost him a fortune.

The party went a bit quiet after the fight. Nobody could top it, apparently, and it was generally considered a good note to finish on. Pat was escorted home in Maltese Joe's Roller. The Perfumed Lady appeared from 'Gawd knew where' just in time to hail a cab and whisk T.C. off to the same hospital as Dave to have his bite treated. She said later that they'd said the human bite, especially Dave's, was so filthy that poor T.C. had to have loads of injections and had to stay in for a couple of days for observation.

'Humph!' was Uncle Bert's verdict. 'Probably looking for signs of rabies.'

'More like he went AWOL for a bit, poor wretch,' Auntie Maggie interjected. 'Can't be easy now, can it? He obviously dotes on her, but still . . .' Then she saw me earwigging and shut up.

Years later, I was to discover that the crowning of the Queen and the fight were not the only things of note to happen on that day. Strictly speaking, of course, the fight took place the day after the Coronation, but that's splitting hairs. The other big event, the one that in many ways was of more immediate importance to us, was the fact that Paulette never did go back to Dave or brassing either.

We never quite understood what made it possible for her to break away, but we were grateful for it. There had been other fights, other women and certainly a good few batterings, but Paulette had always gone back for more. Course, there is a school of thought that says some women enjoy being knocked about and exploited by the Daves of this world. As I grew older, I kept trying to understand why people like Paulette and my mum let men treat them like that. There was a lot of it around our way, with the brasses and their pimps. I needed to understand this because every time my mum turned up covered in bruises, swearing that she'd never let a man do it to her again, I got a little harder, a bit more contemptuous. It was all so different from home where Uncle Bert always treated Auntie Maggie and me with gentleness and respect.

12

We were late getting up on Wednesday but as the morning wore on, various people came in to help tidy the place up ready for opening. Mamma Campanini sent in a selection of daughters and daughters-in-law armed with scrubbing brushes, brooms and floor polish, old Mrs Roberts came and so did Ronnie's missis, Sally. There was a mountain of washing up to do, floors to scrub and tables and chairs to put back where they belonged. Things had got a touch out of hand before Dave and T.C.'s fight was relocated to the street. Varying degrees of hangover made progress slow but steady. I was given a bucket and a wet rag and told to empty the ashtrays, then wipe them round. No wonder no one else was rushing to do it. The smell of wet fag ash – yuk! Everyone else felt too queasy to handle it.

We were all still hard at it when Paulette and Madame Zelda tottered in looking like death warmed up. Everyone was a bit quiet as they worked, so it took me a while to notice that there was something funny going on. They weren't looking at each other, or chatting away as usual. In fact they were distinctly sheepish as they doled out the salt and pepper shakers. What's more, they would start as if they had been electrocuted every time their hands met over the pepper pots or they brushed up against each other in the aisles. You'd think that one of them was plugged into the mains or diseased or something. It was all very weird.

I was busy watching them when Uncle Bert yelled from his kitchen that I could do the honours and open the door for the dinner-time punters. There were plenty of them as people had hung around the pubs and clubs all night, reluctant to stop celebrating. We did a roaring trade in teas and coffees although the punters were a bit leery of actual food, due partly to their hangovers and partly to the fact that they'd blown all their money. It was probably just as well, as Uncle Bert wasn't feeling much like wielding a frying pan anyway.

We were half expecting Charlie Fluck's ugly mug to put in an appearance but he didn't show. Maybe he was still poncing about in Brighton. It wouldn't have mattered a lot even if he had turned up, as it happened, because the Perfumed Lady had disappeared in the early hours with the battered but victorious T.C. in tow. So we couldn't have told him where she'd gone after she'd taken T.C. to hospital even if we'd wanted to, which we didn't.

It didn't take long for life to get back on its well-oiled track once the cafe had reopened. I went back to school on Thursday morning, grumbling every step of the way, but I was all right once I was there. It was always a toss-up. I loved skiving and hanging around with Auntie Maggie and Uncle Bert at the cafe but, on the other hand, all my mates were at school.

We had already flogged the Coronation almost to death in class during the weeks before the big day. The aftermath could have been a bit flat but, as luck would have it, Edmund Hillary and Sherpa Tensing had made it up Everest, which gave us something else to think about, much to the relief of our teachers. We spent a productive time copying sentences, maps and diagrams from the blackboard into our rough books and then we did it all again in our best books. Maybe I'm a bit thick, but I never could work out why we always had to write things out twice like that. I suppose the theory was that if you managed to get it right the first time, chances were you'd get it right and, more importantly, *neat* the second time.

Trust me to show up the flaw in this plan. My second efforts were rarely as good, let alone better, than my first. I'd be bored with whatever it was by the best-book stage and would rush to get it over with so I could begin something more interesting, or at least new. I was always in trouble for scruffy work.

Anyway, Miss Small could tell a good yarn when she felt like it and she managed to get us quite excited about the conquest of Everest. We heard all about previous expeditions being driven back by blizzards, avalanches and lack of oxygen. We oohed and aahed over the poor sods who'd frozen to death in snowdrifts or had stumbled into crevasses, and it seemed only right and proper that Everest should finally be beaten as we entered the New Elizabethan Age. The trouble was, the more I learned about it, the more confused I became. I couldn't quite make out how a New Zealander and a Sherpa who had reached the longed-for summit managed to become *our* brave heroes. Of course, New Zealand was in the Commonwealth, so that probably explained Mr

Hillary's honorary status as a true Brit – but what about Mr Tensing? And if Mr Tensing was a Sherpa, where the hell was Sherp? I looked hard at my atlas. In the end I had to ask and, in case it's been troubling you too, I can tell you that Sherpas come from a spot on the borders of Nepal and Tibet which is nowhere near either New Zealand or the British Isles.

Still, we all found it wildly exciting and me and my mates spent many happy hours scaling the table tombs in St Anne's Square pretending that they were Everest. The paths were transformed into glaciers and the grass was snow. For some reason, I always wanted to be Sherpa Tensing. One of the Chinese kids might have been more convincing, but they all wanted to be Edmund Hillary.

We got bolder as time went on, and used the shed in the corner of the square as our Everest. That idea didn't last long. Enie Smales fell off and broke her leg, the twerp, and ruined it for everybody, and Auntie Maggie threatened to have my guts for garters if she ever heard that I'd been seen prancing about on it again.

The only other thing of note that happened during that time was that Dave came round shooting his mouth off about Paulette getting out of her flat or going back to work. This set the cat among the pigeons. Paulette was desperate to stay on, but she really had had it with Dave and brassing for a living. There were several anxious days with Dave threatening and Paulette getting upset.

It finally came to a showdown about ten days after the Coronation. Dave turned up in a filthy temper, having just come from the dentist. He hated spending his own money, did Dave, and it seems his new crowns had cost him a pretty penny, so he decided that Paulette could pay, one way or another. He had somehow managed to convince himself that the fight was all her fault.

Anyway, there he was trying to get into Paulette's building but Paulette and Madame Zelda had changed the lock on the street door. Dave was standing on the pavement, yelling fit to bust, when Sharky Finn ambled into view. I just happened to be staring out of the cafe window, so I saw it all.

Sharky stopped some distance away and weighed up the situation in a leisurely manner, his head cocked to one side, one eye closed against the smoke from his ever-present, evil-smelling cigar.

As he surveyed the scene, a small smile appeared around the butt in his gob. Then he strolled over to Dave, laid his hand on his shoulder and said something. After a moment or two, Dave shrugged and allowed himself to be led into the cafe by the still-smiling Sharky.

If I had been Dave, I think I would have noticed that smile and it would have worried me as there was something mildly sinister about it. I didn't know the word then but I do now: Sharky's smile was predatory. It was probably how he came to be known as 'Sharky', let's face it, and it was probably what made him a sharp lawyer and an accomplished gambler. As they came through the door, Dave was so busy hooting and hollering, he had no idea at all that he was about to be shafted.

Sharky listened quietly as Dave told us what an ungrateful bitch Paulette was and that if she wasn't planning to go back to work then she could just get the hell out of the flat. Then he got started on how his teeth had cost him an arm and a leg. He was waving both arms about as he ranted, so I checked under the table and sure enough, he still had two legs, so the toe-rag was lying. He went on and on, saying that as far as he was concerned Paulette owed him, he'd sue her to get the money and what did Sharky think?

Sharky took a minute or two to lean back in his chair and consider. Then, eyeing Dave as if he was something he'd found on his salad, he began to speak. 'Don't be a prat, Dave. The girl owes you nothing. You lived off of *her* for years, remember, or are you confusing being a ponce with working for a living?'

Dave began to rise, spluttering that he didn't have to listen to this crap and that if Sharky didn't have anything useful to say, he, Dave, was leaving.

Casually, Sharky hooked his foot around the leg of Dave's chair and gave it a sharp tug. It hit the back of Dave's knees and he sat down again, smartish. By this time I had alerted Uncle Bert to the drama and he was making his way towards their table. Luigi rose quietly from his seat and strolled over to stand in front of the door.

Auntie Maggie muttered in my ear that it might be an idea to get Paulette and Madame Zelda. 'Nip next door, love. Ring Zelda's bell and then stand on the pavement across the road so they can see it's you. Ask 'em to come in here quick. This is going to be good.'

I headed towards the door and Luigi swayed sideways to let me through. Moments later I was back, Paulette and Madame Zelda hot on my heels. Sharky was speaking and Uncle Bert was looming behind the hapless Dave.

'As I was saying, she owes you nothing and if you tried to sue her you'd get nowhere. Chances are, you'd end up being charged with living off immoral earnings before you could spit. In fact, I'll make certain of it if you get up my nose any more.'

'What do you mean, "get up your nose"? What have I ever done to you?'

Sharky smiled that sinister smile of his and blew out a cloud of smoke. 'I'll tell you, Dave, my boy. You've been coming round at all hours of the day and night, upsetting my neighbours and getting on my tits by yelling, threatening and being a general pain in the proverbial. That's what you've done to me – and it stops, right now!'

Dave began to stand up again. 'What makes you think you can stop me?' he sneered. 'If I wanna come round, I'll come round. I'm going to get Paulette out of there and put my Theresa in instead.'

Uncle Bert moved forward slightly, grabbed the chair Dave had pushed back and shoved it hard into the back of his knees. Once again, he went down with a thud. Sharky leaned over the table, eyes glittering and his smile even more sharklike.

'And how do you propose to do that? Surely Paulette's been paying the rent? If I know you, David, and I do, you have never paid a penny. What makes you think *you* can evict her and let the flat to whom you please?' His voice went very quiet. 'What makes you think that you can do that, Dave?'

Dave began to bluster but Sharky held up a hand for silence. 'No, David, I think not. Firstly, you're not the tenant of the flat, Paulette is. I know in the normal run of things that would mean sweet Fanny Adams, but in this case her rights will be observed. Secondly, even if you could get her out, and you can't, you may not move in whoever pleases you. That is not how it works, Dave, my boy, that's not how it works at all. Thirdly, if you are hoping to charm the landlord into falling in with your plans, forget it. The landlord cannot be charmed, bribed or coerced – not by you, anyway. So, if I were you, and thank God I'm not, I'd give in gracefully and piss off and leave her alone. That's what I'd do.'

By this time Dave's face had gone the kind of red that would shame a beetroot. He was beside himself with rage and it took a while for him to find the breath to speak. At last he got it out in a sort of explosive gust that spread droplets of spittle all over those in the immediate area.

'Who the fuck are you to tell me what I can and cannot do?' He leaned forward so that his face was close to Sharky's and bared his teeth, pointing at them with a nicotine-stained finger. 'Look at this lot, just look at 'em. What do you think of 'em – ah, ah? They didn't come cheap. They cost me a fortune, I can tell you. Someone's going to pay and that someone, mate, is going to be that useless cow standing over there.' With this, his yellow digit swung round to point at Paulette, who cowered behind Madame Zelda and tried to look defiant at the same time.

Sharky was unmoved. He took another long drag of his cigar and then peered closely at Dave's teeth, using one slightly grubby forefinger to lift Dave's lip as if he was a horse. Having carried out his inspection, he smiled a long, slow smile. 'You were robbed, my man. They look like chips off a corporation pisshole, and personally I think you'd be better off suing the dentist. As to your other question, I'll tell you who I am. I'm Paulette's landlord. I won the place a while back from Maltese Joe. I'm also the man who, if you ever come sniffing around my door again or bother my tenants in any way – any way at all – will have your arse in the dock so fast your bollocks will drop off. You forget, David, that I'm the man who knows more about your business than you do. Now, haul your arse out of here.

You're getting on my nerves. Luigi, would you oblige and help David to leave?'

Before Luigi could move Dave was on his feet and out of the door.

You could have heard a pin drop after he'd gone. Then into the silence came the sound of Madame Zelda clapping and pretty soon we'd all joined in.

Sharky rose a little from his seat and bowed to the assembled company. What a performance!

13

Needless to say, Paulette stayed put. Dave disappeared but his new girl, Theresa, moved in over the greengrocer's on the corner of Frith Street. She tried to rub Paulette's nose in it for a while, as if she believed that Dave was some sort of prize that she had managed to snatch from her. But it didn't take long for her to cut that nonsense out as Paulette was so obviously delighted with Dave's new arrangement. She had always been distraught in the past when he'd taken up with someone new but this time she seemed genuinely happy to be rid of him.

About a fortnight after Sharky told Dave the news, Madame Zelda asked us and Luigi if we could help her swap floors with Sharky. He had agreed to move into Madame Zelda's so that he would no longer be sandwiched between her and Paulette. This was a lot trickier than it sounds. Although Sharky's possessions were few – a couple of desks, some chairs, filing cabinets and a bed that he used when he couldn't find somewhere else to sleep – Madame Zelda had tons of stuff, including the moth-eaten monkey I loved so dearly. Then, of course, the rooms had to be redecorated as Sharky could hardly conduct his law business surrounded by moons and stars. Ten years of cigar smoke and no paint hadn't done a lot for his place either.

It was a complicated business and there were several planning sessions between Paulette, Madame Zelda and Auntie Maggie. Meanwhile the men hit the woodwork, stating that the women could let them know what they had to do when they had to do it. There was also the ritual of choosing wall-papers and colour schemes. I was allowed to join in with this and we spent many happy hours looking at pattern books and schlepping around various shops.

Then Paulette decided that her place could do with a once-over too as she wanted to get rid of any last traces of Dave and her old job. It was turning into a major operation and Auntie Maggie, who loved to organize, was like a pig in whatever it is that pigs like to be in. Uncle Bert was less enthusiastic as he said he'd be the poor sod who did most of the work

– well, him and Luigi. He also said you could bet your life that Sharky would be nowhere to be found when the time came, and he was right about that too.

We decided to do Sharky's and Madame Zelda's rooms at more or less the same time and to leave Paulette's until they were finished. We had to do the work at a weekend because Sharky and Madame Zelda really needed to be open for business on weekdays, and so did we.

As soon as we'd closed the cafe on Saturday afternoon, we were hard at it. We began with humping cases and boxes down the stairs and into the cafe for storage. Next came the furniture. Finally, when the places were empty, all the women, including Ron's missis, Sally, and the odd Campanini, went to work with scrubbing brushes, cloths and sponges. I was given a scraper and charged with removing some of the old wallpaper. It was great! I was allowed to get as filthy as I liked. Once one room had been prepared, Uncle Bert would move in with his wallpapering table, Luigi and Paulette would begin the painting and the rest of us would move on to prepare the next room. By Sunday evening, Madame Zelda's old place had been transformed into Sharky's new offices and looked really smart.

Auntie Maggie, Madame Zelda and Paulette had decided on a masculine no-nonsense Regency stripe for Sharky's waiting room-cum-secretary's office-cum-bedroom. Auntie Maggie donated some plants for the window sill so that Muriel – Sharky's long-suffering secretary and longest-serving mistress – would have 'something better-looking than Sharky' to brighten up her working hours. Muriel worked three days a week, typing up the stuff that Sharky felt was safe enough to be committed to paper. Rumour had it that she also kept secret files, stuffed full of more dubious information, as insurance in case Sharky's more bloodthirsty clients were to decide that he knew too much. But back to the decorating: the inner sanctum, Sharky's office, boasted pale grey wallpaper with stripes in blocks of three, a thickish dark grey one flanked by two narrow maroon ones. I thought it was very boring but everyone else thought it was smart. Muriel was delighted with her new surroundings but was gloomy about the prospect of keeping them nice, Sharky being something of a world-class slob.

Madame Zelda's was next. Her consulting room ws made more or less the same as before and I had a lovely time drawing and then painting stars, moons and suns on the freshly painted dark walls. I loved the glittery gold and silver paints and Madame Zelda even let me write my name in the corner, saying that an artist should always sign her work. My chest was puffed with pride for days. I was an artist like the ones who made chalk pictures on the pavement or set up their easels in the squares and showed off their pictures on the railings on Sundays.

When Madame Zelda had lived downstairs, her second room had been a sort of bed-sitting room, cluttered with things that I had grown to love. This time, the second room was transformed into a living room with pretty flowered wallpaper, a table, chairs both upright and easy, a radiogram and a settee. But there was no bed and no stuffed monkey clinging to his lamp. Where was Madame Zelda going to sleep, I wondered. More importantly, where was the stuffed monkey? I began to ask searching questions but Madame Zelda and Paulette looked flustered and eventually Auntie Maggie told me to mind my own business. It worried me though, especially the fate of the monkey.

Last but not least, we began work on Paulette's rooms. We didn't have time that first weekend, being up to our eyebrows getting Sharky's and Madame Zelda's working rooms sorted. The second weekend was taken up with finishing things off on the first two floors, so it was well into July by the time we got to the top floor. This time the decorating was much simpler as all Paulette's stuff could be moved downstairs to Madame Zelda's and, because Paulette no longer worked from home as it were, it was OK to work on the two main rooms at the same time. Once again I had a field day ripping off wallpaper, and Luigi found a screwdriver and removed the mirrors from the walls and the ceiling. Once the rooms were stripped and prepared, Uncle Bert went into action with his wallpapering kit.

By the time we'd finished, it was really hard to imagine that the place belonged to the same person. Instead of all the froth and frills of her brassing days, Paulette had plumped for a jungle in her bedroom. We got up really, really early one morning and raided Covent Garden for some likely-looking plants to enhance the effect. In fact we managed to get so many that Paulette had to flash a bit of cleavage to encourage one of the blokes to wheel her instant jungle home on a cart. I am thrilled to say that the monkey reappeared at this point. Instead of clambering up a standard lamp, he seemed to be about to swing from the corner of the room with the aid of an artificial creeper. I helped to make this by cutting out leaves from dark green, glossy paper and attaching them to a length of rope, which after much work on both our parts looked really convincing. We were so taken with our success that we produced a whole lot more and pretty soon the ceiling was festooned with the things. Later, during my school holidays, Paulette and I haunted junk shops searching out stuffed birds, small animals, artificial flowers and butterflies so that they could lurk among the dense foliage that had replaced the ceiling mirrors. We had a wonderful time.

While we were all working up there, though, I was getting more and more confused. Paulette's living room disappeared and another bedroom took its place. It took me a while to work it out. Finally, the light dawned. Of course! The second bedroom was for Madame Zelda.

14

Hooray! The summer holidays had arrived and school was over until September. We kids poured out of those school gates on the last day of term, hopping, skipping and whooping our joy, completely oblivious to the fact that within a few short weeks we'd be kicking our heels and whining that we were bored. Come September, it'd be quite a relief to get back to the familiar routine once again. Still, on that day in late July when we were officially free, getting back to school was the furthest thing from my mind. I was one of those lucky few whose birthday fell in the summer holidays and I was wild with anticipation. I was always spoilt rotten on my birthday.

It was round about this time that I noticed Charlie Fluck lurking in doorways again, odd eyes peeled. I had a love-hate relationship with phrases such as 'keeping your eyes skinned' or, worse still, 'keeping them peeled'. If I wanted to make myself feel sick, I'd give the idea serious thought and within seconds I'd turn a fetching shade of green. I could see it all: first, I'd select a really sharp knife from Uncle Bert's kitchen. Then I'd test the edge by splitting a hair with it like they did in those cowboy or gangster pictures. Next, I'd pop the eye out, holding it firmly between thumb and forefinger, preferably with the business side turned away so that it couldn't stare reproachfully at me. A vicious little stab with the point of the knife would get things started, then slowly and deliberately I'd run the knife around the eyeball so it peeled like an apple. Careful concentration would be necessary to avoid slicing my thumb or cutting too deep. The trick would be to get the skin off in one long, satisfying spiral.

Another option was the orange method, where I'd gouge a bit out with a thumbnail and then peel the skin away, segment by segment, although if my orange-peeling experiences were anything to go by this would be a lot messier. You may be wondering why I would want to feel sick. Well, it was a very handy knack if there was a visit to the dentist in the offing, for instance, or a tables test at school.

Anyway, I saw Charlie Fluck and reported it

straight away to Uncle Bert. I knew the Perfumed Lady was far from reliable but chances were she'd put in an appearance some time around my birthday, and there Charlie would be, lurking. He could lurk for England, could Charlie. He wasn't particularly good at not being spotted but he seemed able to lurk for hours and hours without getting bored and wandering off. As Auntie Maggie said, he should have been born in a doorway as they seemed to fit him like a glove. Every now and then he'd flit to another one, just to ring the changes, but he always kept the cafe in clear view.

Uncle Bert was not unduly concerned but he told me to keep an eye on the bleeder while he tried to get my mum on the blower. Luckily it was morning, so if she was home she'd still be in bed. He nipped next door to Sharky's and came back grinning from ear to ear. She was home, apparently, and 'compos mentis for a change', whatever that meant. She had completely forgotten being told about Charlie on Coronation Day and how we'd sent him off to Brighton, but then she forgot a lot of things when she was on the bevvy, did my mum. According to Auntie Maggie, this was probably the point, but I didn't really understand that. Anyway, we had managed to establish that her name really was

Cassandra Loveday-Smythe, poor thing, so we knew Charlie was on the right track but we didn't know why. It had been arranged that she'd come over, heavily disguised, and get a good look at Charlie and see if she recognized him. Perhaps, if she knew him, she'd have some idea as to why he was trying to find her. She might even confront him, but that decision could be left until she'd given him the once-over.

For the rest of the morning there was an air of expectation as we waited for my mum to turn up. Even Mrs Wong seemed interested. It was hard to tell of course, but I don't think she liked that Charlie either. Dinner time came and went and still no Perfumed Lady.

As the hot, sticky afternoon wore on, it became apparent that there'd been some kind of hitch. Uncle Bert nipped next door to ring her again, but this time there was no reply. Charlie had disappeared into the Coach and Horses for half an hour at dinner time, but apart from that he hadn't left his post.

'You'd think he'd need a pee at least, wouldn't you?' Auntie Maggie asked no one in particular.

There was still no sign of the Perfumed Lady when we closed the cafe for the day, but Charlie was still there, leaning against a wall, eyes peeled.

* * *

Charlie took up his vigil again the next day and the next but my mum didn't show or answer her phone. She seemed to have disappeared into thin air yet again. Uncle Bert and Auntie Maggie were philosophical; after all, it wasn't the first time she'd failed to show up as promised and it undoubtedly wouldn't be the last. I was a bit anxious myself. If she forgot to come and see Charlie, chances were she'd forget my birthday as well – a far more serious matter as far as I was concerned. She'd never forgotten before, although sometimes she'd been a bit late.

I asked Auntie Maggie what she thought had happened to her.

'I 'spect she was ambushed by a vat of gin some-where between here and there. Don't you worry, love. She'll show when she sobers up. Meanwhile, we've got a birthday to organize; I just wish I could remember whose.'

My wail of protest brought a wink and a huge grin to her beloved round face and I was reassured.

I can remember vividly what I got for my birthday that year because I still treasure it today. It was a truly beautiful doll's house lovingly built by Uncle Bert and decorated by Auntie Maggie. Uncle Bert had spent months and months working on it in secret during lulls in business while I was at school and after I had gone to bed. They had hidden it in the cellar, happy in the knowledge that nothing on this earth would induce me to go down there on my own. Madame Zelda, Paulette and the Campaninis were in on the secret and each contributed something to it.

Uncle Bert had made a three-storey, Georgian-type house, not unlike some of the buildings round Soho. The front was covered in paper that looked just like real bricks and there were steps up to an elegant porch and a panelled door with a handsome fanlight above. The whole frontage was hinged so that it opened to give access to the interior. The first two floors had a hallway with two large rooms on each side, and there were six little attic rooms on the third floor. These were for the servants, my auntie Maggie said.

There was a kitchen, complete with a tiny black range, a white butler's sink and a built-in dresser with shelves and cupboards. The floor was covered in the lino that we had in our own kitchen. The living rooms were much more luxurious, with wallpaper, carpets, fireplaces and tiny electric lights that really worked. The battery that operated them was housed in a sort of lean-to attached to the back of the building. I was mesmerized by them and knackered the battery in double-quick time by switching them on and off constantly. Luckily, Uncle Bert had anticipated this and thoughtfully provided a spare. Uncle Bert had an uncanny knack of thinking just like a child when the occasion demanded.

Auntie Maggie, Madame Zelda, Paulette and Mamma Campanini also did me proud. Madame Zelda provided a lovely little settee and two armchairs for the living room. Paulette gave me a bedroom suite, complete with a four-poster bed, a wardrobe and a dressing table. Mamma Campanini's contribution was a hamper full of food for the kitchen. The bright pink ham joint and the leg of mutton were made of plaster, and so was a minute loaf of bread complete with bread board. There was a bottle of wine, made of real glass, and packets labelled sugar, flour, suet and tea. The tinned stuff looked just like the real thing – tomato soup, baked beans, red salmon and peaches. There were even tins of custard, Oxo cubes and cornflour in miniature. Sheer magic!

Auntie Maggie had really gone to town. One of her parcels contained the dinkiest tea set you ever saw and another held a set of copper pans for the kitchen. Yet another was full of minute rag rugs, sets of curtains, a quilt for the four-poster and lamp-shades for the torch bulbs suspended from the ceilings. She had made all of these things herself and it's a wonder that she didn't go blind, what with the tiny little stitches and all. When I think of it now, I am staggered at just how much thought and love went into it all.

15

Auntie Maggie couldn't wait to get me up on the morning after my birthday.

'Come on, slow coach, get them lazy bones out of that pit,' she chided. 'You've got ten minutes to get washed, dressed and ready for anything. Your breakfast is almost on the table. Come on now, quick as you can. Downstairs in the caff in ten minutes, ready to wrap your laughing gear round your breakfast and open your parcel.'

The word 'parcel' got my attention all right. I was out of my bed and halfway to the door before I'd even opened my eyes. I loved a good parcel. Let's face it, who in their right mind doesn't? There is something special about a package that comes through the post. I was down those stairs, still damp behind the ears and with my blouse hanging out, in five minutes flat. Uncle Bert and Auntie Maggie were already ensconced at our table and there, by my place, was a large parcel wrapped in brown paper and secured with stout string. Uncle Bert eyed me over his *Daily Mirror* as I skidded to a halt and flung myself into my chair.

'Sleeping Beauty has arrived at last, eh? I do hope your early rising won't damage your health, my dear,' said Uncle Bert from around his pipe. 'I'll just get her ladyship her breakfast, shall I? It's keeping warm in the oven.' He heaved himself to his feet as I began to wail about opening my parcel first, then having my breakfast.

Auntie Maggie was adamant. 'Not on your nelly, my gel. Breakfast first, then the parcel. These things are always better for a bit of anticipation, really they are. Anyway, you might get bacon fat or fried egg all over what's inside and that wouldn't do at all.'

I opened my mouth to protest, caught the gleam in her eye and knew that resistance was useless. I snapped my mouth shut and looked sullen instead.

Auntie Maggie ignored my expression and pointed to the stamps plastered above my name and address. 'Look, love, them's French stamps and the postmark says Paris, which is the capital of France as I'm sure you know. Now I wonder who can be sending you stuff from foreign parts?'

I knew she didn't expect an answer. Guessing games were one of Auntie Maggie's specialities and her face always fell if you guessed too quickly.

'P'raps it's that lady who had her head chopped off for saying "Let them eat cake," ' I suggested, completely forgetting that I was sulking.

Auntie Maggie looked interested. 'What lady was that then?'

'It was that queen. Mary something or other.'

'Marie Antoinette,' supplied Uncle Bert as he returned with my breakfast.

'Mary who?'

'Not Mary, Marie,' he said, gesticulating wildly with my plate so that the egg was dangerously close to slipping down the back of Auntie Maggie's neck. 'Marie Antoinette,' he repeated in his best Maurice Chevalier voice as he plopped my plate down in front of me. 'Eat. Now where was I? Oh yes, Marie Antoinette, French Queen during that Revolution they had over there. Got her head chopped off, as Rosie so rightly says, along with all them other French aristos. Well, those who couldn't leg it fast enough, that is. Did I ever tell you two that my mob originated in France? We was supposed to be French aristocrats with a chateau, land and everything.'

Auntie Maggie and I exchanged long-suffering looks and rolled our eyes at each other. He was off again!

'Yes, dear, you have told us, hundreds of times,' Auntie Maggie cut in quickly before he could hit his stride. 'The thing is, if this Marie Antoinette had her head chopped off, how could she find her way to the post office? Eat your egg white as well, Rosie, there's a good girl. And your crusts. It'll make your hair nice and straight, just like Kathy's. So this queen of yours couldn't make it to get the stamps without her head, now could she, let alone write the address? Or does she carry her head under her arm like Mary Queen of Scots?'

Uncle Bert shook his head. 'You've got a point there, Maggie, my love, I've never heard that she carried her head about, so I reckon not. Now who else is there? We don't know anyone French, apart from Frenchie from the pub and he wouldn't be sending our Rosie parcels, would he?'

I was munching steadily as they pondered the problem and batted ideas back and forth. They were still at it when I'd finished and it was a moment or two before I could attract their attention. 'Can I open it now? Can I?'

They pretended to consider and then grinned and nodded. Uncle Bert cut the string neatly with his penknife, just by the knot, and rolled it up into a tidy, small ball. We never threw string away, or brown paper for that matter, so I had to open the parcel with care. There was no point in giving it a thorough feel first because whatever it was, was obviously in a good, stout box, so the shape would give no clues. I unwrapped the paper and folded it very carefully. Inside was an ordinary cardboard box with some French writing but no picture. Auntie Maggie began to tease Uncle Bert: if he was a Froggy, could he translate it for us, she asked.

To my horror, he snatched the box from my grasp and pretended to read the inscription. 'Le Blanc, that means "the White", snails and frogs' legs to the gentry. Two dozen prime limbs of the amphibian and two dozen living snails.' He raised the tips of his fingers and thumb to his pursed lips and, in an expansive Gallic gesture, made a kissing sound. 'Delicious!' he announced, as we squealed in disgust.

He handed me back my parcel and at last I was free to open it. Auntie Maggie hastily removed my greasy plate and dumped it with a thud on the next table. They both leaned forward as I fumbled with the box.

When I finally got it open and peered inside there was an envelope addressed to me, another addressed to Auntie Maggie and Uncle Bert, and loads of smaller parcels, individually wrapped in coloured paper. There were red, blue, green, yellow and purple ones. I removed the envelopes, handed theirs over and gently tipped out the rainbow packages. I recognized the style: the Perfumed Lady had remembered my birthday and, what's more, she had remembered just how much I loved to open parcels. Of course we'd known it was from her all along – she was the only person we knew who was likely to send me parcels from Paris. One or two local bookshop owners got stuff sent from Paris, it's true, but not through the post. No, those parcels came with shifty-eyed men with wide lapels, shiny hair and lots of gold rings. The same ones that stood about hissing on street corners offering punters post-cards of naked ladies.

I opened each parcel slowly, savouring the joy of it. It seems that the Perfumed Lady had been in on the great doll's-house conspiracy and each tiny parcel contained another contribution. There was a family of dolls – mother, father, a little girl, a little boy and a baby in a cot that rocked. There was a collection of minute toys for the children to play with, including a spinning top that didn't spin on account of being too small, a titchy doll's pram, a football and a playpen for the baby. Best of all was the rocking horse. It was a dappled grey with a scarlet saddle and reins; its eyes were wild and its tail streamed behind it.

I was thrilled to bits and itching to get upstairs so that I could put the people into my house and get playing, but Auntie Maggie insisted that I open my card first. It was a picture of a little girl with huge eyes, all dolled up in fancy frills and ribbons. Inside the Perfumed Lady had written, 'Happy birthday, darling. I hope to see you soon, love Mummy,' with lots of kisses. Yuk, 'Mummy'! Nobody called their mum 'Mummy' except those squirts in the films or Enid Blyton books.

My eyes must have been pleading because Auntie Maggie grinned and said, 'Go on, then.' I went. Later, they told me that the Perfumed Lady was sorry that she'd been away for my birthday but that something had come up. I am sorry to say that I didn't mind a lot. I had my presents, and the most beautiful doll's house in the world.

16

The other big event of the summer, besides my birthday, was our holiday. Auntie Maggie had a younger sister, Flo, who had moved to a place Uncle Bert always called 'Aggie on Horseback' and she had invited us to visit her.

'Where the hell is Aggie on 'Orseback when it's at home?' demanded Madame Zelda when a letter came from Flo soon after she'd moved away. I was glad she'd asked because it had been worrying me too, but when I questioned Auntie Maggie she was vague and said it had something to do with sailors but she was blowed if she could remember what.

'It's what the sailors call Weston-super-Mare, Zeld. It's down in Somerset, by the sea,' Uncle Bert explained.

'All right, I'll go for that. But why *do* sailors call it

Aggie on Horseback? I see the horse bit, but who was this Aggie person?'

Uncle Bert put on his best schoolmaster's voice and puffed his chest out ready to deliver his words of wisdom. He liked to tell people things. 'One Agatha Weston, Zeld. Famous for being good to sailors.'

'Hmph.' She snorted. 'Paulette's been good to loads of sailors in her time and I don't see no places named after her.'

'Not that kind of good, Zelda. For starters, *she* gave *them* money, not the other way round.'

'Oh, I see,' gasped Madame Zelda as she and Auntie Maggie rocked with laughter. I wasn't at all sure that *I* saw but I laughed anyway, not wanting to be left out.

Auntie Flo had kept in touch regularly every week since she'd moved away with Sid, her second husband. Johnny, her first, had copped it in the war, having stood on a landmine. Auntie Maggie had never liked Johnny as she suspected him of being a womanizer and very poor husband material altogether. On hearing the news of his demise, she'd had real trouble keeping the satisfaction out of her voice. 'He'd always spread hisself a bit thin but never from here to kingdom come before,' she stated. Of course, she was very careful not to let Auntie Flo hear her views. Auntie Flo had never complained to anyone about her Johnny and Auntie Maggie didn't want to hurt her feelings now that Johnny's philandering days were over.

Auntie Maggie and Uncle Bert had much more time for Sid, who was a travelling salesman, and were genuinely pleased when Auntie Flo and he tied the knot. They gave them a fine old wedding bash at the cafe and then the happy couple moved to the seaside and the boarding house run by Sid's mum. The idea was that Auntie Flo would help with the boarders and Sid would carry on travelling with his ladies' corsets.

Much to everyone's astonishment, including Auntie Flo's, she and her mother-in-law got along fine together right up until the old girl died. Then Uncle Sid and Auntie Flo inherited the boarding house and now they were in the middle of doing it up. Auntie Flo's plan was that we would go down for a holiday and help with the refurbishments at the same time.

'Oh good,' groaned Uncle Bert when Auntie Maggie read the invitation to him. 'Some holiday, I don't think. Up to our armpits in scrubbing and decorating, I'll be bound.'

'Stop your moaning, Bert Featherby. The change'll do us all good and anyway Rosie's never seen the sea, have you, love?' I opened my mouth to answer, but she ploughed on. 'She's my sister, Bert. She could do with our help, and I for one don't mind giving it.'

Uncle Bert rolled his eyes at me and patted Auntie Maggie's substantial knee reassuringly. 'Keep your hair on, Maggie, my love. Your sisterly devotion does you credit. I was only saying. Of course we'll go and we'll give her a hand, if that's what you want. Anyway, it's about time we had a holiday and it's time the rug-rat here saw the briny. Write back and tell 'em we'll be down straight after Rosie's birthday.'

In the event, it was decided that Madame Zelda and Paulette should come too and we were all wild with excitement. I had never been out of London before and I had no idea what to expect.

We had my birthday party on the Saturday, after the cafe closed. My mates used to fall over themselves to get to a bunfight thrown by Auntie Maggie and Uncle Bert. Uncle Bert would always finish off by entertaining us with his famous magic tricks and every kid would leave with some sweets he just happened to 'find' nestling in their ears or even in their nostrils. The 'nose sweets' never failed to bring forth disgusted cries from the party-goers but it didn't seem to put anyone off eating them. Sweets were a really big deal in those days because they were still on ration, but Uncle Bert could always get them when the need arose, rationing or no rationing – another bit of his magic.

This particular birthday party went with the customary swing, although we finished up a little more smartly than usual on account of leaving for Aggie on Horseback the next day. We had packing to do and a couple of Campanini girls were coming by to receive their last-minute instructions. They had agreed to help Mrs Wong take care of business while we were away, and Luigi had promised to keep an eye on things.

We were still downstairs, clearing up the cafe, when there was an agitated rapping on the door. Uncle Bert shouted that we were closed, but the rapping came again.

'Who is it, Bert?' Auntie Maggie yelled from the kitchen.

'I dunno. Some old gent I've never seen before. Bugger off, mate. Can't you see we're closed?' He was just tapping the closed sign and glaring at the old man when I, being a nosy little sod, came out to investigate.

'Wait a minute, Uncle Bert. That's Mr Herbert from the bookshop. You know, the one I told you about. Hello, Mr Herbert. What are you doing here? Can you let him in, Uncle Bert? I know him, honest I do. It's him who chooses all those books for me that you like so much – *The Wind in the Willows* and all that.'

Uncle Bert unlocked the door, apologizing to Mr Herbert as he did so. 'I'm sorry, mate. I didn't know you was a friend of our Rosie's. Any friend of hers is a friend of ours. Come in, why don't you, and take the weight off.'

Mr Herbert bustled in beaming, and with his hand out to shake Uncle Bert's to show there were no hard feelings.

'Hello, Rosa, my dear, how nice to see you again. How are you and how is dear Cassandra? I don't seem to have seen either of you for a long while. This must be . . . er . . . Uncle Bert. How do you do, sir? A pleasure, sir, a real pleasure. And this is your good lady?' He bowed stiffly to Auntie Maggie who had appeared in the kitchen doorway, wiping her hands on her pinny. She blushed a fetching pink and invited him to sit down and have a cup of tea.

The chat was idle for a bit. Uncle Bert and Auntie Maggie established that Mr Herbert had run the bookshop for the better part of thirty years and that he lived above his shop. They compared notes on living and working in the same place and concluded that, despite some drawbacks, it was a jolly good thing. The main problem, as they saw it, was getting away from work. They agreed that a change of scene now and then was essential. Auntie Maggie talked about our holiday with Auntie Flo, her sister, which led on to Mr Herbert knowing a 'local chap' once, years ago, who'd had two daughters, Margaret and Florence, and it turned out from that that he'd known Auntie Maggie's dad quite well. They had played chess together at a club that met on Tuesdays in a room above the Coach and Horses.

'Of course he was a senior member and it was some time before I had the privilege of playing him,' Mr Herbert said. 'A very fine player, Mrs Featherby, very fine. Quick, too.'

Auntie Maggie beamed, eyes misty for a second, then she sat up with a jolt. 'Hang about! You're not "young 'Erbert", are you? I remember my dad coming home in a terrible temper because "that young 'Erbert" had beaten him, not once but three weeks on the trot. Was that you?'

Mr Herbert fidgeted for a bit and looked modestly at the ground before owning that he and young

'Erbert were, in fact, one and the same. 'I should like to add, Mrs Featherby, that your dear father did go on to beat me several times after that. I think my game confused him for a bit – until he got used to my style of play, that is.'

'You're being too modest, Mr Herbert. My dad thought you was one of the finest chess players he'd ever met. What's more, you was really good to him when he couldn't get about no more after his stroke. Played by post, you did, never missed a turn in all them years. He loved those games, Mr Herbert, he really did. He was in the middle of one when the bomb hit 'em; he'd got me mum to write down his next move and everything. I know 'cause I was going to post it for him but he just wanted to think about it a bit longer, to make sure. Said he couldn't slip anything past you. They got clobbered that very night.' Auntie Maggie sniffed slightly, fished out a huge, snowy handkerchief from the pocket of her pinny and blew into it mightily.

There was a moment's silence as we all thought about Auntie Maggie's mum and dad, killed by a direct hit during the Blitz. The spot where their house had been was a sort of car park now. It was the place where the pack of stray dogs hung about waiting for Auntie Maggie to step out in her best moleskin coat. It was also where the 'ten bob and find your own railings' class of working girls plied their trade, according to Paulette. I couldn't quite see why they were called this because there weren't any railings. They'd been taken away for scrap to help with the war effort, or so Auntie Maggie said when I asked.

Uncle Bert was the first to come back to the present. 'It's been fine wandering down Memory Lane with you, Mr Herbert, but you've not told us to what we owe the pleasure.'

'Yes, yes, of course. Foolish of me to get side-tracked. It's about Rosa's mother, Cassandra; I suppose you have no notion as to where she is at present, do you?'

I had my mouth open ready to say 'Paris' when I felt the gentlest of nudges against my ankle and snapped my gob shut. I was being reminded not to answer questions about people we knew until I had some idea as to why the questions were being asked in the first place.

As ever, Auntie Maggie came straight to the point. 'Why do you want to know, Mr Herbert, if you don't mind me asking? We're not in the habit of passing on information, as I'm sure you will understand.'

Mr Herbert became a little hot and bothered and assured Auntie Maggie that he understood perfectly; it was just that he had an urgent message for her.

'Can we ask who the message is from?' Uncle Bert asked. 'Of course, if you'd rather not say, we understand.'

'No, no, my dear chap. There's no big secret. It's from Cassandra's aunt Dodie. She just wishes to tell Cassandra that some unpleasant type called Fluck, of all things, is sniffing around and asking all sorts of questions. Dodie feels that Cassandra should be warned, that's all.'

Uncle Bert took the opportunity to explain that we knew Charlie Fluck and that he had been hanging about the cafe, on and off, since before the Coronation. Mr Herbert got flustered at this news and tutted a fair old bit.

Again Auntie Maggie was the first to pose the question. 'How come Cassie's auntie Dodie knows you, Mr Herbert? We'd already figured that you knew our Cassie fairly well, from what young Rosie told us about you. But how does her auntie Dodie know to get in touch with you? Perhaps you'd better explain a bit?'

'My dear lady, of course. It must seem very odd, this perfect stranger on your doorstep asking questions. Allow me to begin at the beginning. Dodie Loveday-Smythe and I are very old friends, yes indeed. It must be more than fifty years ago now . . .' And he was off, weaving this wonderful story about his childhood somewhere in the country. Dodie was there too, playing in some orchard during the long, hot summer holidays with Mr Herbert and another bloke called Alex. As they grew older, hide-and-seek in the orchard gave way to tennis parties and croquet on the lawn. It sounded lovely, but then the Great War took all the young men away, including Mr Herbert and this Alex. 'Poor Alex bought it pretty early on, I'm afraid. Dodie and he were to be married, you see. Tragic!' Mr Herbert shook his head and looked sorrowful. There wasn't a dry eye in the house.

It turned out that this Dodie person was my mum's dad's sister, which, according to Auntie Maggie, made her my great-aunt. It was all very confusing. Anyway, the upshot was that Charlie Fluck had been a chauffeur with my mum's parents; my granny and grandpa, according to Auntie Maggie that is. I couldn't take it all in. Suddenly I had all these great-aunts, grandpas and grannies I knew nothing about and it made me feel a bit funny, so I switched off for a while and thought about something else. I was just running through all the things that I wanted to take away with me to Aggie – my new doll's house naturally, all my dolls, teddy of course, a book or two and maybe the odd yo-yo – when I became aware that Mr Herbert was making moves to leave.

He was standing by the cafe door having his hand pumped enthusiastically by Uncle Bert, who had obviously taken to him. They were assuring each other that they would do their level best to get hold of the Perfumed Lady while keeping an eye out for the repulsive Charlie. Uncle Bert promised to report to Mr Herbert when we got back from the seaside. A final handshake and Mr Herbert was gone and we were free to get on with the packing.

It was a bit of a blow to discover that my suitcase wouldn't hold my new doll's house and that it, and most of my toys, would have to stay at home. It was an even greater blow when Auntie Maggie broke the news that my suitcase would be filled with such boring items as knickers, socks and shorts. I had been looking forward to showing off my best toys to Auntie Flo, Uncle Sid and the locals.

17

I didn't have much time to think about this mystery family I had tucked away somewhere because we had a lot to do before I went to bed that night. It was just as well really because thinking about them still made me feel strange. Mr Herbert had left with our assurances that we would pass on his message as soon as we could, but he said he understood completely that we couldn't guarantee her co-operation. The Perfumed Lady was, after all, what Auntie Maggie called 'a free spirit', and there was just no telling where a free spirit was likely to end up or what it was likely to do.

'Especially if the "spirits are free",' Uncle Bert was quick to point out and they all laughed. Yet again the joke missed me. Grown-ups had a funny way of talking, I reflected, and sometimes, especially when kids were around, they appeared to use a sort of code.

Meanwhile, Charlie seemed to have disappeared, though Mr Herbert had shown great interest in the fact that he had been lurking, on and off, for some time and assured us that he'd tell Aunt Dodie. It was also agreed that we should give him Auntie Flo's address just in case he needed to contact us in a hurry. I wasn't included in the discussions that followed his departure and I couldn't even be bothered to eavesdrop. I was just too knackered and over-excited to cope with any serious skulking with my ear to a keyhole. It had been an eventful day – a birthday bash then Mr Herbert's visit.

All the talk about my shadowy other family and lurking Charlie had rattled me quite a bit. For once I was downright thankful to get to the sanctuary of my bedroom. I was busy with my doll's house when Auntie Maggie came to tuck me in. 'Who got evicted then?' she asked, pointing at the small heap of discarded dolls beside the house. She plonked herself heavily on the floor beside me and peered into the tiny rooms. 'And who are these that got to stay?'

'That's you, that's Uncle Bert and that's me there.' I pointed to each one in turn. 'Then there's Madame Zelda, Paulette and Luigi waiting in the parlour.'

'I see. Well, it's time we sent the visitors home and tucked you up in bed. You've a big day tomorrow and you'll want to be fresh. Give us a hand up, there's a good girl.'

I heaved and tugged and Auntie Maggie gasped and spluttered. Soon we were giggling too hard to do anything useful and Uncle Bert had to come and help Auntie Maggie back on to her pins. By the time I was between the sheets and had been well and truly kissed good night, I was feeling several shades happier than I had been. I didn't have to count the roses on my summer curtains for long before I was sound asleep. After all, I had never been away from home before and the holiday seemed to be far more exciting than anything to do with my mum and Charlie Fluck.

There was a time, in our part of Soho, when most of the money earned by the local brasses found its way one way or another into the pocket of Maltese Joe. Either the girls worked directly for him or for one of his henchmen; or they lived and worked in flats owned by him; or their pimps blew all their profits in one of his many spielers. A spieler was a gambling club and there were loads of them around in those days. In any event, the girls were ready, willing and able to relieve the eager punter of any filthy lucre that might be burning a hole in his wallet. This made Maltese Joe a very rich man.

Now I never really knew the ins and outs of it, but Uncle Bert had a special relationship with Maltese Joe. We didn't pay protection, for instance. Occasionally, when rationing bit too deep, a swift word with Maltese Joe sent a tide of spivs to our door, flogging everything you can possibly imagine. There was one bloke, who had connections with the meat market, who could provide a whole cow on or off the hoof!

The morning we were to leave for Aggie there was a loud insistent hammering at the cafe door. Madame Zelda and Paulette had already arrived, so Auntie Maggie said to ignore it – we were busy with a last-minute wrangle about the ratio of books, toys and knickers in my suitcase and I was losing. The hammering did not stop, so in the end I was despatched to get rid of whoever it was.

I opened the door and there stood Frankie, one of Maltese Joe's boys, dressed in a chauffeur's uniform, complete with cap and jodhpurs. I looked around for his horse but all I could see was this huge, gleaming motor car.

As soon as Frankie saw Auntie Maggie and Uncle

Bert hove into view behind me, he whipped off his cap and bowed low. 'Maltese Joe sends his compliments and says the Roller is at your disposal until I have to collect his old mum from Mass at eleven. He understands that your train leaves at ten o'clock, which gives us plenty of time. Can I help you to load your bags and that?'

Uncle Bert was the first to recover from the unusual sight of Frankie done up like a dog's dinner, bowing and scraping as if we were royalty. Me and Auntie Maggie just stood there with our gobs open, trying to take it all in.

'Thank you, Francis, my man. Can I tempt you with a cup of something while we sort ourselves out? Then you can load the bags. Come in and sit anywhere that takes your fancy. What would you like – tea, coffee?'

'That is most civil, Mr Bert, sir. Tea would be fine, thanks. Plenty of milk and sugar, if you please.'

Auntie Maggie went to make him his tea and the rest of us saw to the last-minute closing of bags and the hunting up of stuff we thought we might have forgotten. Finally the cases were all collected in a mound near the cafe door, ready to be stowed by Uncle Bert and the new, improved, toadying Francis.

Just as we were ready to go, Luigi showed up to

wish us a good holiday and to collect the spare set of keys. He took one look at Frankie's outfit and began to take the mickey something alarming. There were references to the three thirty at Epsom and somebody called Lady Chatterley liking to be ridden by a bit of rough. When Frankie began to mutter something about hoping that 'that bleedin' little wop had a good dentist and if he didn't shut his cake'ole right now, he'd never ride *anythin'* again, not even a number 11 bus', Uncle Bert decided enough was enough and calmed them both down.

Shortly after that, we all (except Luigi of course) climbed into the Roller and drew away from the cafe in style. Madame Zelda made us all laugh by waving out of the window as if she was the Queen. We were on our way at last.

I found Paddington Station a bit overwhelming. The noise seemed deafening as it echoed around that cavern of a building. Metal wheels screeched on rails and put my teeth on edge. Steam engines puffed and wheezed like asthmatic dragons as they got up a head of steam ready to move out or let go of the excess as they slowed to a stop. The smell of coal and smoke reminded me of the depths of winter when everyone had their fires going. It was strange to smell coal fires on a hot day in July. I gripped hold of Auntie Maggie a bit tighter while the others bustled about buying tickets, finding the train and organizing the bags to disappear into the luggage van. Frankie got into the spirit of the thing again after his ruck with Luigi and had porters running in all directions while he played the part of the faithful retainer who had finally found some lower orders to boss about.

While Uncle Bert and Frankie organized the porters, Auntie Maggie, Madame Zelda, Paulette and I went looking for our seats. I had such a tight grip on Auntie Maggie that I can still remember the look of my knuckles, all white and pointy. I didn't trust that train not to belch and hiss boiling hot steam at me. Then, when we found our carriage, there was a huge canyon between the platform and the train. It was terrifying – I could see right down to where the rails gleamed dully in a deep, dark hole. A vision of missing my step, slipping and being trapped down there flashed across my mind and I was speechless with horror. I almost dragged Auntie Maggie's arm out of its socket as I pulled back from the yawning chasm. Then a giant swooped down, hoisted me into the air in an elegant arc and landed me in the doorway of the train. 'There you are, little lady, safely aboard,' he boomed, and my saviour was gone. It was like being rescued from the dentist's, a tables test and a bollocking from Auntie Maggie all in one. My relief was so intense that I burst into racking sobs. I was immediately enveloped in a perfumed chest and clucked over all the way to our seats.

I was overwrought, my auntie Maggie said, and I suppose I was.

18

Apart from getting on to the train, I really enjoyed the journey down to Aggie on Horseback. Auntie Maggie had decided that if she and Uncle Bert were taking a break from catering, it could 'bloody well start in the Pullman car, so sod packets of sandwiches and flasks of tea'. It was therefore agreed that any refreshments we required could be provided by British Railways and hang the expense.

First off, though, before we got to the Pullman, we had to negotiate those bits where the carriages were joined to each other. I don't know if the stuff they used to hold it all together was canvas or leather but it was pleated like a giant concertina or the sides of a pair of bellows and seemed pretty flimsy to me. The floors were even worse, with metal plates that moved from side to side or ground together when the driver slung out his anchors. I was even less happy about these joins than I had been about the pits of hell at Paddington. In the end I had to be carried over them by Uncle Bert, who was kind enough to make no comment. I was lucky like that; neither Uncle Bert nor Auntie Maggie were of the persuasion that the way to encourage a frightened kid was to jeer at it, in public or in private. Some parents do that, don't they – shame children into doing things that terrify them? I remember being really shocked the first time I saw someone do that to their child. Even *I* squirmed with humiliation. Anyway, I'm thrilled to say that my lot never did that sort of thing to me.

Once we had safely negotiated what seemed like hundreds of those bloody joins, we finally made it to the comfort and safety of the Pullman car. I was enchanted with the whole thing. I loved the little lamps on the tables, which came complete with dear little lampshades with bobbled fringes; I liked the etched glass that proudly proclaimed *Pullman*; I liked the waiters in their stiffly starched white jackets with spotless tea-towel things draped smartly over their arms; and I was particularly impressed with the way they poured the coffee from an elegant silver-metal pot with a long narrow spout. They managed not to spill a single drop – and I was watching like a hawk – even as the train lurched and thundered through the countryside.

Once we were back in our seats, I was mesmerized by the passing scene. I had never been out of London before, or if I had I had been far too young to notice, so I was staggered by the sheer expanse of green, and bowled over by the sight of real sheep and cows. I also saw these great big grey birds that were standing around on one leg in a field. I jumped up and down, clamouring to be told what they were. Uncle Bert and Auntie Maggie exchanged baffled looks and asked Madame Zelda if she knew, but she shook her head.

Paulette supplied the answer. 'They're herons,' she said firmly.

'How do you know they're herons?' demanded Madame Zelda suspiciously. 'When have you ever seen a heron?'

'I used to see 'em hanging around the waterworks near us when I was a kid. Anyway, I like birds and I used to get books out the library when I was at school.'

She blushed slightly in the face of the gob-smacked expressions the other three grown-ups turned on her. Here was a side of Paulette we had never suspected.

She obviously felt that we deserved a fuller explanation. 'It's their feathers, the colours and that. Some of 'em 'ave the fanciest feathers you ever saw, 'specially some of them tropical ones like all them birds of paradise. It's called plumage.' This last was brought out in a voice of quiet pride.

'That's why you done our room out like a jungle, I s'pose, with them stuffed parrots. I half expect to land in bird shit every time I get up for a pee in the night. Thank Gawd they're stuffed is all I can say.' Madame Zelda shook her head, still a little stunned. 'You never said you liked birds. Well, you live and learn, don't you? You think you know a person inside and out and then they go and surprise you.'

She gave Paulette an almighty dig in the ribs. Unfortunately it was delivered with such good-natured force that Paulette fell sprawling into the lap of a thin, wispy woman sitting in the corner. This sent the rest of us into gales of hearty laughter as Paulette struggled to right herself. The wispy woman, however, was not amused. She gave a thin smile at the chortled apologies and stared fixedly out of the window, trying to pretend she wasn't earwigging every word any of us said. Nosy old bag!

We heaved a sigh of relief when she got out at a place called Swindon and we had the compartment to ourselves. It felt like being let out of school on a bright summer day.

Auntie Flo and Uncle Sid were at the station to meet us. It was difficult to see that Auntie Maggie and Auntie Flo were sisters. Auntie Flo looked tiny next to Auntie Maggie, but then so did everybody. Uncle Bert and Uncle Sid shook hands in a manly way while Auntie Maggie and Auntie Flo launched themselves at each other with hugs, kisses and glad cries of joy. Madame Zelda, Paulette and I sort of hung about, a bit spare for a moment or two, then it was our turn to be greeted. Uncle Sid grabbed me under the armpits and swung me around so high and fast everyone and his brother got a clear view of my drawers. Luckily they were sturdy ones. He restricted himself to handshakes when it came to Madame Zelda and Paulette, I noticed.

After this flurry of greetings, our bags were collected from the luggage van and we piled into Uncle Sid's shiny black Riley. I had to sit on Auntie Maggie's lap in the front with Uncle Sid, and Paulette sort of sprawled across Madame Zelda, Auntie Flo and Uncle Bert in the back. Luckily we didn't have that far to go as the boarding house was placed neatly between the station and the 'front', as

Auntie Flo called it. Now, the only 'fronts' I'd ever heard of were when Auntie Maggie warned me not to slop my milk down mine, or when I went to the front of the class or the front of the queue. I think it was the first time I was aware how many meanings some words have.

Pondering this great fact kept me busy all the way to the boarding house, so I didn't really notice what Aggie on Horseback looked like that first day.

19

I distinctly remember my first sight of the sea. It was such a disappointment. All I had ever seen before were pictures and they tended towards the dramatic – you know the kind of thing: huge Atlantic rollers crashing onto jagged rocks that poke out of the spume like shattered fangs. I suppose I was thinking of the pictures of the terrible floods earlier in the year, when the Queen went to see the damage and told everybody how sorry she was.

At Aggie there were no rollers, no broken teeth, no spume – just miles and miles of flat muddy-looking sand. Even the sand was hard to see, what with the hordes of holidaymakers milling about, jostling for a spot to pitch their towels. You needed to take a picnic with you if you set off towards the actual water for a paddle; you could be gone for days, according to Uncle Bert. I was much more impressed with the donkeys and, later on, candyfloss. I fell in love with the donkeys immediately. I loved their warm, cosy smell; I loved their coats and their long, expressive ears; but most of all I loved the feel of their soft muzzles and the way they blew through their noses when they were pleased to see you.

Uncle Sid went zooming up in my estimation when I discovered that one of his drinking pals was a bloke called Harry with a string of his very own donkeys. I was ecstatic! Once I got my bearings, I was down on that beach day after day, getting under Harry's feet and adoring Daisy, Hazel, Midge, Madge, Smudge and Budge with all my heart. Well, nearly all of it, as some was still reserved for Auntie Maggie, Uncle Bert, Madame Zelda, Paulette, Luigi, Mamma Campanini, Auntie Flo and Uncle Sid.

Soon, great chunks of my pocket money were going on bags of carrots and before long I was a dab hand at feeding, grooming and swinging on girth straps. You may not know this, but donkeys have a really lively sense of humour. In fact, there is nothing a donkey likes better than a good laugh. Sometimes they'll stand nonchalantly on a person's foot, nailing them to the ground. Then they pretend they can't hear the anguished cries even though they're coming from a gob not six inches from their enormous lugs. They'll gaze into the distance, thinking deep thoughts. In the end, only a bribe of a sugar lump, a piece of apple or a carrot will shift 'em. Carrots are best because they don't rot teeth or cause colicky guts. As you can tell, I've got to know quite a lot of donkeys since I first fell in love with Harry's little mob.

Talking of Harry's little mob, one of Hazel's favourite jokes was to puff out her belly as far as it would go when her saddle was being put on. The joke was that when anyone tried to mount, the saddle slipped round and dumped the rider in a confused heap on the wet sand. I swear that when this happened she actually smiled, showing rows of big, blunt, yellow teeth and acres of shiny gums. If the joke was particularly successful, then Hazel would let out a huge belly laugh. She'd fling back her head and utter a series of ear-shattering hee-haws. Then the others would join in, donkey laughter being as catching as people laughter. I swear the resulting racket could be heard clearly in the Charing Cross Road.

It was difficult to be angry with Hazel when she was having such a good time but you had to be really firm to stop her from pulling the saddle trick.

First you had to tug the girth strap tight, then you had to knee her in the gut (don't worry, if you did it right it didn't hurt a bit) and pull the strap a bit tighter until you were sure that all the air was out of her. Even so, she still managed to work the odd trick by holding on to her last gasp. The best thing to do then was to pretend to finish, wander off to do something else, then give the old girth another hefty tug when she was relaxed and not expecting it. Needless to say, Hazel was my favourite. I liked her style.

Donkeys were yet another subject on which Paulette and I were in full agreement. I realize now, of course, just how lucky I was to have a grown-up for a friend who also enjoyed dressing up, doll's houses, Murder in the Dark and donkeys. If Hazel was my favourite then Budge was Paulette's. She said he reminded her of Madame Zelda and I knew what she meant. Budge also had a sense of fun, but you wouldn't want to cross him – oh no! Budge had a kick on him that could send the beefiest of fellas into the middle of next week, no messing. Harry reserved Budge for the lads on the beach who had had one or two too many and could do with 'a good kick up the arse'. Like Budge, Madame Zelda also had a way with stroppy blokes.

*　　*　　*

While I was haunting Harry and friends down on the front, the others were busy working on the boarding house. Once or twice we went on day trips to local beauty spots but I don't really remember what they were called. At first, Paulette would accompany me to the beach in the mornings to keep an eye on me and make sure I wasn't too much of a pest. At dinner time I'd be prised loose from Harry and the mob, and if I was in luck either Auntie Maggie, Uncle Bert or Madame Zelda would take me back again in the afternoons. Within a few days, though, I'd made friends with a girl called Penny who was staying just up the road. After that, she'd call for me in the mornings and I'd go to the beach with her and her family.

Our temporary life in Aggie on Horseback had settled rapidly into a contented rut when a telegram arrived to shatter the calm. It was from Mr Herbert, saying that if we were agreeable he would like to bring Dodie Loveday-Smythe to meet us. He suggested the following Thursday and asked if we could let him know whether this was convenient.

That dinner time the entire household sat down to discuss this turn of events. Naturally, Auntie Flo and Uncle Sid had to be filled in up to date and then everyone fell to speculating about the reason for the visit. That it had something to do with the Perfumed Lady, Charlie Fluck and my mysterious family was obvious, but exactly what we couldn't say. The whole thing made me feel a bit anxious, especially as I could tell that Auntie Maggie and Uncle Bert were worried too.

Later, when I was supposed to be in bed asleep, I overheard Auntie Maggie talking to Madame Zelda. 'We can't *not* see 'em, Zeld. It might be urgent, but I'm not happy. As far as I know, Cassie never told her mum and dad about Rosie so what happens if this Dodie woman tells them, eh? Answer me that. It could have all sorts of consequences. Then again, if Cassie trusts her, maybe we should too. It's all so tricky.'

'Why don't you play it by ear, Maggie? Why don't you send our Rosie to the beach as usual, and me and Paulette can go with her and take her out for her dinner at the chippy if needs be. Then, if you think the old girl's all right, you can let her meet Rosie. And if you don't, well, tell her Rosie's out for the day and maybe she can meet her another time with Cassie. How about that?'

'It's a good plan, Zeld, I'll give you that. But I'm still not happy. I can't help thinking it would be better for all of us if we'd never had anything to do with Cassie's lot. After all, she buggered off and left 'em, and she must've had her reasons.'

'But you know what teenage girls are, Maggie love. They might just have had a silly row. You never know, her folks might be real charmers.'

'But look at the state of her now, Zeld. You can't tell me that her mum and dad had nothing to do with that because I won't believe you. She was just a kid when Bert found her, about seventeen. She was cold, she was hungry and she was four months gone with Rosie and at her wits' end. She only tried to sell herself to Bert for the price of a meal and a warm bed. Poor little cow. Course, being an old softie, Bert brought her home to me to be looked after and the rest you know. The point is, she didn't know Bert from Adam and he could've raped or murdered her, but she didn't seem to care. She could've tried to flog herself to that toe-rag Dave or worse. Now then, what sort of parents let their kid get in a state like that and then don't stand by her, you tell me that?'

'Gawd, Maggie, why do you think them un-married mothers' homes do so well? Because poor little cows like your Cassie are always getting slung out for being in the puddin' club, that's why. She wasn't the first by a long chalk and she surely won't be the last.'

'I know, I know, but I find it hard, that's all. I just wish I knew what to do for the best. Bert thinks we should see 'em and so does Flo.'

'I think you should see them too. They might want to make it up with Cassie and Rosie, you never know, in which case you should give them the chance. And if they are up to no good, better we should know about it so we can all defend ourselves. I'd make sure Rosie wasn't around, not at first, just to be on the safe side, but if you reckon this great-aunt of hers is kosher, then you can always arrange for her to see Rosie when it suits everyone, not just her.'

At that moment I heard someone coming along the passage and decided the time had come to retreat swiftly to my bedroom, so I never did hear what their decision was.

Events suggest that Auntie Maggie took Madame Zelda's advice, however. The following Thursday everyone was on edge at breakfast. As soon as the last crumb hit my tonsils, I was scrubbed, combed and whisked off to a place called Clevedon by Madame Zelda and Paulette. All I can remember about Clevedon is that there were no donkeys, no candyfloss, no chippy that we could find – and no miles and miles of wet mud. Instead there was a lovely front so I got to see proper sea at last, waves and all. I even swam in it and so did Paulette and Madame Zelda. In fact, when I managed to forget about THE VISIT, I had a good time.

20

It was almost five o'clock in the evening by the time Madame Zelda, Paulette and I got off the bus from Clevedon. We must have made quite a picture as we trailed down the road, hair all claggy and stiff with salt. Our clothes were rumpled and mine, at least, were grubby too. Just to add to the general joys, I'd managed to lose a sock, so my feet were bare in my sensible brown Clarks sandals.

The combination of bare feet, salt and leather had caused blisters on both my heels, so I was limping a bit as I mounted the steps to Auntie Flo's. Paulette and Madame Zelda had stopped to admire a rather dashing low-slung silver sports car parked at the kerb outside.

They were just wondering who on earth it could belong to when Auntie Maggie flung open the front door. She let out a screech as she saw the state of me and whisked me upstairs before I could say a word. Next thing I knew I was up to my ears in hot water, shampoo and soap. Auntie Maggie was babbling as she scrubbed. I had rarely seen her so strung up.

'Gordon Bennett! The state of you. What *have* you been up to, you mucky little tyke? I see, that's why your mush is so grubby – candyfloss and general grime, lovely! It's set like concrete. It'll take sandpaper to scrape it out of your eyebrows. We can't let her see you like that, now can we? She'll think we don't know how to look after you. Now you keep washing while I find you some clean clothes. What have you done with that sock? Oh never mind, don't try and answer. It doesn't matter and you'll get soap in your gob if you try and speak. Now, what can I put you in? I know, the pink – you look lovely in the pink. Ah, Paulette! Can you keep scrubbing while I go and sort out some clobber for her? Back in a tick.' And she was gone.

An anxious Auntie Maggie was unnerving and I was getting flustered. Who was this ogre who mustn't see me looking grubby? What would she do? Would she snatch me away?

Paulette was soothing. 'I've just met 'er, love. She's a right old duck. She's getting on like an 'ouse on fire with everyone so don't you worry. That's just your auntie Maggie getting in a state. Of course she wants you to make a good impression. She's proud of you and she wants you to look your best. Take no notice. Anyway, you did spread that candyfloss about a bit, now didn't you?'

All the time she was speaking she was making with my flannel. Pretty soon I was deemed ready to get out of the bath to be dried. Auntie Maggie bustled back in just as Paulette was wrapping me in a huge white bath towel. She had my pink frock, socks, knickers, shoes and a hairbrush with her. I knew the signs and gritted my teeth and thought of England. Well actually, I gritted my teeth and thought about Daisy, Hazel, Midge, Madge, Smudge and Budge.

Eventually, the ordeal was over and I was ready to be presented, or so Paulette assured Auntie Maggie. 'She looks gorgeous. For Gawd's sake, Maggie, calm down. You're getting poor Rosie's knickers in a right old twist with all your fussing. She seems a nice old girl and she's going to like our Rosie no matter what state she's in. Now come on, the pair of you, and bugger off. I want to wash me hair.'

We met Madame Zelda on the stairs. She was coming up as we were going down. 'She's a right old goer, ain't she, Maggie? We had a good old gas about that ex-husband of mine. She said she didn't trust him from the start and I told her she wasn't far wrong. By rights, his ears should be on fire by now and settin' off his barnet while they're at it. That Mr Herbert's a nice old geezer an' all. Where's Paulette?'

'She's in the bathroom, Zeld, washing her hair. Yes, she does seem all right, and you wait till I tell you what she's been telling us about your Charlie and Cassie's lot. I've found out more about our Cassie's past on one afternoon than I have in all the years I've known her. How she managed to keep her gob shut about it, I'll never know. Still, that'll have to wait till later. Right now, we'd better get little missy here introduced to her great-aunt Dodie toot bleeding sweet. She'll think I've spirited her away somewhere. And Zeld, I hope you don't mind me saying so, dear, but you don't half look a sight. What have you been doing, the lot of you? No, tell me later. Right now there's a dear old trout looking forward to meeting this young trout here.'

It seemed an awful long way from the bathroom to the sitting room. Auntie Flo had taken to calling it 'the lounge' for some reason but I always thought it was an ugly word and never really took to it. It still seemed an awful long way away and I was getting more and more nervous with every step. At last we reached the sitting-room door, which was closed. Both Auntie Maggie and I hesitated once we got there; I was treated to more tweaking, prodding and smoothing and then, as one, we took deep breaths and Auntie Maggie opened the door.

I don't know what I was expecting, someone who looked like Queen Mary, I think – sort of grey and stern and well upholstered. But Great-aunt Dodie was not at all like that. To begin with, she was very, very tall, like a man. She had what Auntie Maggie diplomatically called 'big bones'. In other words, she had enormous hands and feet and great wide shoulders but absolutely no spare flesh. Her back was ramrod straight, her jaw was square and firm, and her nose was long, thin and hooked like the beak of an eagle. The whole effect would have been very intimidating if it wasn't for her eyes. They were large and the most extraordinarily clear blue and they twinkled with amusement. I was to learn later that anger made them glitter menacingly, but on that first meeting they twinkled. Paulette called the colour 'periwinkle blue' as if she knew what she was talking about, so I suppose she did. The only other thing I noticed was her hair. It framed that extra-ordinary face in a soft halo of pure white. The soft white hair said 'dear old lady' but her body and face said 'Don't mess with this one. She's as tough as old boots.'

'Go on, Rosie, give your great-aunt a kiss. Don't just stand there.' Auntie Maggie gave me a little push, but I was rooted to the spot. I wanted to know what she would do first, before I committed myself. Her voice was loud, penetrating and very, very posh. You know the expression 'speaks with a plum in her mouth'? Well, this one spoke with the whole tree.

'Don't bully her, Mrs Featherby. She doesn't know me from Eve. I expect she's shy. Let's face it, first sight of me is enough to put the wind up anyone. Been known to see off a bunch of Afghan tribesmen in my time. Came across the blighters lying in ambush in the Hindu Kush. The villainous devils took one look at the old physiognomy and decided discretion was the better part of valour. Great bandits, the Afghans, even the locals always travel in caravans for safety. Bloody good horsemen too, I'll say that for them. They've got this game, bit like polo, except they play it with a dead goat. Ferocious so-and-sos often kill each other over this bloody goat, but you've never seen riding like it, take my word.

'So, little one, please don't trouble yourself about me. You just carry on, Rosa, and see what you make of me first. If you decide I'll do, then we can get acquainted. Meanwhile, Mr Featherby, you were telling me about that little snot, what's his name? Clunt, is it?'

At this, everyone exploded into gales of laughter – everyone, that is, except me and my great-aunt. We both looked bewildered.

'Did I say something? Oh, of course, of course, it's Fluck, isn't it. I always balls it up. You were telling me about Charlie Fluck and how you sent him to Brighton – so clever of you.'

I settled down on Auntie Maggie's lap with my thumb in my mouth and was quite happy to watch and listen for a bit. Mr Herbert kept casting me small, reassuring smiles and once he even winked. It didn't take me long to realize that despite her appearance, that booming voice and her cut-glass accent, Great-aunt Dodie was indeed 'a right old duck' as Paulette had said.

21

Time was marching on and there was still no sign of my tea. At last I could stand it no longer and whispered in Auntie Maggie's ear about the state of my belly.

'Now, Rosie, don't whisper, it's rude. Flo, what are we doing about food? Rosie here tells me she's running on empty and I'm feeling a little hollow myself.'

Auntie Flo looked flustered and muttered something about not being sure she had enough ham to go round. Great-aunt Dodie leaped to her feet and made moves to leave, apologizing all the while.

'I am *so* sorry, I quite lost track of time. Of course everyone's hungry. Archie and I will take our leave now. Thank you so much for your hospitality. Come on, Archie, shake a leg.'

Uncle Bert held up an imperious hand. 'Don't be daft. So there's not enough ham? That's no reason to leave. It seems a pity to break up the party now. How about going to Coffin's for a slap-up plate of fish and chips? That's if you like fish and chips of course.'

Great-aunt Dodie beamed, showing a set of teeth Hazel would have been proud of. 'Like fish and chips? I should say I do. Remember, Mr Featherby, you're talking to a woman who has not only eaten sheep's eyes with the Bedouin but has survived the food at Cheltenham Ladies' College. Now *that* is no mean feat, I can tell you. What d'you say, Archie? Fish and chips at Coffin's? Then I suggest a stab at plan B.'

'That sounds *most* pleasant, Dodie dear,' Mr Herbert said. 'I must say that the establishment's name adds to its allure. I wonder if they have to put up with a lot of cannibal jokes? I expect they do, poor things.'

I must have decided that Great-aunt Dodie was all right because before anyone could stop me I was demanding to know what 'plan B' was.

Auntie Maggie looked embarrassed, although I could tell that she and everyone else wanted to know. 'Shoosh, Rosie, don't be so rude. It's none of our business what plan B is.'

'Don't trouble yourself, Mrs Featherby. Of course the girl's curious. Archie and I had three possible plans, Rosa. Plan A was to come and visit you all, stay a polite interval and then motor back to Bath and my home in time for supper. Plan B was to come and visit you, find an hotel, and then, if you're game, see you all again tomorrow. Plan C is in case you're busy tomorrow and we have to amuse ourselves by pootling about a bit before returning to Bath.'

Uncle Sid was adamant. 'This is a boarding house, Miss Loveday-Smythe. We've got plenty of room, if you don't mind the smell of paint. It's not as bad as it was, although I could just be getting used to it.'

Everyone began talking at once, except me and Mr Herbert. I was too faint with hunger to argue the toss and kept tugging at Auntie Maggie's dress until I got her attention.

'Yes, love. How about we all talk it over while we're wrapping our laughing gear around some cod and chips? Me and Rosie here are about to fade away from lack of grub.'

It didn't take long to walk to Coffin's and get all nine of us seated. To my relief, the table was soon groaning under the weight of huge plates of fish and chips, teetering piles of bread and butter and steaming cups of tea.

Between mouthfuls, it was decided that once we'd eaten we'd all return to Dunroamin for what Madame Zelda called 'a good old chin-wag and piss-up'. There was general agreement to this plan.

'Plan D,' I yelled through a mouthful of chips and everyone laughed, I don't know why.

Dunroamin was the new name that Uncle Sid and Auntie Flo had chosen to go with the new paint, curtains and lino at the boarding house. Uncle Sid said it might bring them luck and enough business so that he could stop travelling in corsets and settle down with his Flo. I had been trying to work out what 'travelling in corsets' meant for some time. I thought it meant that Uncle Sid was like Sugar Plum Flaherty who lived round the corner from us. Sugar liked to dress up like a lady and walked around in high heels, stockings, smart dresses, a blond wig and make-up. I was a bit confused, though, because Uncle Sid never looked like Sugar. I'd never seen him in a dress even, let alone a corset. In the end I asked Paulette what 'travelling in corsets' meant.

'Bless you, sweetie,' Paulette answered. 'Your uncle Sid doesn't *wear* dresses or corsets. He *sells* corsets to shops, that's what it means. He travels about in his nice car, flogging corsets to shops who then flog 'em to ladies and sometimes to people like Sugar or Freddie the Frock, but mostly to ladies.'

Once the last crumbs had been demolished, we all traipsed back to Dunroamin via the boozer on the corner. Uncle Sid and Uncle Bert had insisted on paying for everyone's fish dinners, saying it was their duty to feed their guests. This made Great-aunt Dodie and Mr Herbert very determined to lay in the drinks. There was a spirited discussion about this but Great-aunt Dodie stood her ground. We were despatched home to sort out some glasses and she and Mr Herbert disappeared into the off-sales bit of the pub. Ten minutes later they came staggering in with two wooden crates. One was filled with bottles of beer, lemonade and orange juice. The other had whisky, gin, port and several packets of Smith's crisps. They didn't have fancy flavours in those days, just plain with a little, dark blue twist of paper with the salt in it.

Our party was soon in full swing. Madame Zelda, a glass of gin in one hand and a small cheroot in the other, settled down happily with Mr Herbert and soon they were nattering away twenty to the dozen about books, the occult, Soho and the war. Paulette,

Uncle Sid and Uncle Bert were at the piano, Paulette singing quietly with Uncle Bert accompanying her and Uncle Sid listening and sometimes joining in with the singing. I was sitting with Auntie Maggie, Auntie Flo and Great-aunt Dodie because the talk had got on to funny food and I was dying to know how you ate sheep's eyes. I must have decided that I liked my great-aunt because before long I was happily ensconced on her lap.

When there was a brief gap in the conversation, I whipped my wrinkled thumb out of my mouth to ask about the sheep's eyes. I was quite disappointed to hear that they were put into a stew whole. However, I cheered up when Great-aunt Dodie told us about the Bedouin custom of giving them to honoured guests because they were a delicacy. Of course, the next thing I asked was whether you swallowed them whole or cut 'em up. Auntie Flo told me I was a revolting little tyke but Great-aunt Dodie said it was a good question. She was just about to answer it when Mr Herbert, who'd had a few by then, demanded that she gave us a tune because Uncle Bert was taking a rest. Auntie Maggie suddenly noticed the time and said it was way past my bedtime and that was that. I was whisked off to bed and missed the rest.

I felt cheated because I knew it was highly likely that I never would find out about the sheep's eyes. Personally, I think you'd have to cut 'em up, because they might get stuck in your throat otherwise.

22

The evening must have gone with a swing, because no one was up next morning when I padded downstairs in my nightie with the pink rosebuds on it. I tried to be quiet but I fell off the chair I'd climbed on to reach a cup for my milk. The crash woke Auntie Flo who tottered into the kitchen looking bleary. I babbled an apology for the broken cup but she was casual about it.

'Don't worry, petal, accidents happen. Want some breakfast? I expect your belly thinks your throat's been cut. Egg on toast do you? The eggs come from Sid's cousin who's got a farm round Blagdon way. One egg or two? Boiled, poached, fried or scrambled?'

I wasn't used to making this particular decision for myself. I usually had what everyone else had, so it took me a while to make up my mind. I plumped for two and scrambled. I liked the way Auntie Flo scrambled her eggs; she added some stuff that looked like grass but smelt a bit like onions. She called it chives and it grew in the back garden. She handed me the big black kitchen scissors and asked me to get some while she made some tea.

'Me mouth feels like a wrestler's jockstrap and I won't feel better until I've had a cuppa or six,' she said as she opened the door for me.

Auntie Flo and I spent a companionable hour, drinking our drinks – tea for her, milk for me – and tucking into scrambled eggs on toast. Well, I tucked in and she nibbled the odd dry crust because she said she felt a bit seedy.

I liked my auntie Flo. She'd lived with us for a bit before she married her Sid and moved away. In those days she'd been known to everyone as 'Scarper Flo' on account of being a bookies' runner for a while. She'd become a runner after her Johnny had got himself blown to bits. She had to earn her living somehow and wanted to stay at home to help Granny look after Gramps, who'd had a stroke. There were no farms or munitions factories in Soho, so the choices were limited. In the end, Tic-Tac Mac offered her a job as a runner and she turned out to be really good at it.

Auntie Flo earned the 'Scarper' on account of her turn of speed when being pursued by the coppers. It was illegal, as Uncle Bert explained, to place a bet anywhere except on the race course, but what working man or woman could afford to go to the races every time they wanted a bet? It was daft and, as my auntie Flo pointed out, rich blokes could place a bet by sitting on their fat arses and getting a lackey to telephone their bets through. Or they went to proper gambling clubs where they could play cards and the doorman would place their bets for them. She said it just wasn't fair because *they* had the time and the money to go to the races and the rest of us didn't, and I believed her. Anyway, that's why the people who took bets from the punters were called runners – they had to be able to leg it when the need arose. Scarper Flo soon became a legend with other runners, bookies, punters and police alike and everyone was sad when she gave it up to marry her Sid. The local coppers reckoned that all the exercise she gave them kept them in mid-season form. No one ever managed to catch her, which must have been some kind of record in itself. Most runners expected to get caught now and then and kept a fund to pay their bribes or fines – mostly it was bribes because round our way the coppers saw it as a valuable addition to their wages.

Once we had breakfasted Auntie Flo decided it was best to try and get the others up. We chatted about my Great-aunt Dodie as we boiled the kettle for everyone's morning tea. In fact she'd been the main topic of conversation all through our breakfast. We decided that we liked her; that she was very definitely a bit of all right, and that she was a welcome addition to our little tribe.

Auntie Flo told me how my great-aunt had kept everyone amused with her travel stories and how she and Mr Herbert had taught everyone to play a game called backgammon. They'd had to use a set of draughts, a bit of old sheet with the board drawn on it and some dice. She said she'd teach me later because it would be good practice for my sums. Then she loaded seven cups and saucers on a tray and headed upstairs with the teas. I followed behind so that I could knock on doors and help her deliver them. It came as a bit of a surprise to me to discover that Mr Herbert and my great-aunt were in the same room. Auntie Flo said not to worry about it as he had been servicing the old girl for years. I wasn't sure what servicing meant but Auntie Flo said I didn't really need to know. What I couldn't understand, though, was how the pair of pink knickers came to be hanging from the light fitting in their room. Auntie Flo told me that I didn't need to know that either, but she was laughing as she told me so I knew she wasn't cross.

After we'd delivered tea to Great-aunt Dodie and Mr Herbert, we moved on to Madame Zelda and Paulette's room, then Auntie Maggie and Uncle Bert's and that left just one lonely cup on the tray for Uncle Sid. Once everyone was up, we sat around the long kitchen table discussing our plans for the day. I was all for going to visit the donkeys and Great-aunt Dodie said she'd like to come too. Mr Herbert wanted to look around for bookshops and the rest were happy to spend the morning recovering from the after-effects of the night before.

Great-aunt Dodie proved to be a mine of information about horses and donkeys. She took to Harry's mob straight away and understood completely why Hazel was my favourite. She had a long technical conversation with Harry concerning the dietary requirements and habits of your average donkey. I noticed that Harry behaved very differently when he was speaking to my great-aunt. He had a sort of 'cheeky chappie' manner with the punters but with her he was quiet and serious. I think that was when I realized that she really wasn't like the rest of us. Not only was she posh, which I'd already realized, but she had an air of authority that she and everyone else took for granted – a bit like the headmistress at school, only much, much more so. No wonder Afghan tribesmen legged it rather than face her down.

After we had communed with Hazel and co. for a bit we headed back to Dunroamin via the candyfloss place. Great-aunt Dodie took my auntie Maggie aside for a moment, there was a brief discussion and I heard Auntie Maggie say, 'I don't know, Dodie. Why don't you ask her?'

I just had time to register that their relationship had moved on to a first-names basis when, to my utter astonishment, that imposing woman hunkered down so she was more or less on my level.

'Rosa dear, how would you like to come for a spin in the car? I know someone not too far from here who keeps a farm with horses and I thought, as you love donkeys so much, you might like to meet them.'

I cast a hasty glance at Auntie Maggie to see what she thought of this plan. She smiled at me and nodded slightly, so I knew it was all right with her. So I nodded too, although I have to say I was a bit shy about going off with a woman I hardly knew.

I needn't have worried as what followed was one of those days that linger in the memory for ever. It was a turning point in all sorts of ways as Great-aunt Dodie and I forged a bond that was to be a source of pleasure and strength to us both. We discovered that we shared a great love of the horse. I already knew I loved donkeys but I hadn't yet met many horses. I'd seen them dragging milk and coal carts about; I'd seen them all done up for the Queen's Coronation; I'd seen them in Westerns at the pictures, but I had never been introduced to one before. But what really happened that day was that Great-aunt Dodie helped me to discover my real mother – not the poor, drunken, frightened woman who reeled into the cafe now and then but the person she had been before she was wounded.

Naturally, grown-ups being what they are, Great-aunt Dodie and Auntie Maggie had extensive discussions about when we'd be home, the provision of grub and whether or not I should take a cardie or even a coat, given the English climate and all. Eventually I was skipping down the steps of Dunroamin and standing beside the silver car that was still parked outside our front door. I later learned it was called a Lagonda. Whatever it was called, I discovered that I liked speed and I loved open-topped cars. Great-aunt Dodie's driving was fast and assured and before long we were twisting and turning along the country roads.

As we drove, my great-aunt kept up a running commentary on our surroundings. I hadn't realized, until that day, that my mother had been born and brought up in Somerset. First off, we stopped outside a house with an orchard and a large garden.

'Cassandra's school chum, Lilian, lived there,' my great-aunt told me. 'They were great friends until the family moved to Brazil. See that big apple tree there, the one next to that gate? Well, your ma fell out of that when she was about your age. Bit clear through her tongue, poor thing. Claret everywhere. Still, she was a brave little soldier; didn't cry that much. Would you like to see where she was born, your ma? Well, off we go then. It's not that far.'

We sped between hedgerows for what seemed ages to me and finally came to a halt in front of an imposing pair of wrought-iron gates. To the right of the gates was a building that Great-aunt Dodie called a lodge but that looked just like a little house to me.

We waited for a moment or two, then she heaved a sigh. 'I'd better knock them up, otherwise we'll be here all day.'

She got out of the Lagonda and strode over to the door of the lodge and hammered on it. A small, round, grey-haired woman with a bun answered the knock. I heard her cry, 'Miss Dodie!' in surprise but I didn't hear the rest of the conversation because they were too far away. Shortly my great-aunt returned to the car and the little round woman opened one of the gates. We drove through and the gate was closed behind us.

'Thank you, Mrs Saunders,' Great-aunt Dodie called. 'Just showing my godchild the old homestead.' And with that she put the car into gear and, with a cheery wave, we pulled away.

We drove in silence while I took in the scene. We were on a drive lined with horse chestnut trees. On either side there were lawns bounded by high brick walls clothed in espaliered fruit trees. In later years I was to learn that crops of apples, pears and even peaches were to be had from these peculiar trees that looked as if they had been crucified. In front of the walls, wide herbaceous borders provided a riot of summer colour. Old cottage-garden favourites including hollyhocks, golden achillea, pink phlox, purple Canterbury bells and the majestic spikes of blue delphiniums vied for attention. At the front of the borders, close to the ground, heartsease and pansies turned their pretty little faces to the sun. There was a smell of lavender on the light breeze. I was enchanted. We relied on the royal parks and Covent Garden market to supply our floral displays.

We negotiated a right-hand bend and there before us was a large, old house. It wasn't really anything like as big as Buckingham Palace but it looked it to me. I was overawed and my eyes must have looked like saucers. We drew up at the bottom of a short flight of stone steps guarded by two stone greyhounds. The house was square and symmetrical. Whoever built it was really keen on the numbers three and nine. There were nine windows on each side, three on each of the three floors. The windows themselves were large and had nine panes of glass, three rows of three. I know this because I had recently mastered my multiplication tables up to the six times and so it was easy to work out.

I was still hanging about at the bottom of the steps when Great-aunt Dodie tugged on a long metal rod to the right of the panelled front door. I heard the jangle of a bell. While we waited, I took in some more details. I was fascinated by a sort of shell thing above the door. You couldn't really call it a porch because it wouldn't shelter anyone much or stop the rain from dripping down your neck, but it was pretty. There was a wisteria growing up the left-hand side of the house, although I didn't know what it was called then. It was obviously very old because its trunk was gnarled and twisted like an arthritic finger, only much, much bigger. Later, when we were inside, I saw an oil painting of the house and in it the wisteria was in full bloom. It looked wonderful, like a blue waterfall cascading over that half of the building.

At last, a small figure dressed in black answered the door. She had a chain hanging from her dress belt and attached to it was a large bunch of keys. She took one look at my great-aunt and her old face broke into a wide smile, rearranging the thousand wrinkles into a new pattern.

'Miss Dodie, what a surprise. Why didn't you say you were coming? Mr Charles is up in town. He will be so sorry to have missed you. Come in, come in.' She stepped back from the entrance to make room and then she saw me. 'And who is this? Come, child, don't be afraid, I shan't eat you. In you come.'

Despite her reassurances, I was not at all sure she wouldn't eat me or keep me a prisoner or something equally awful. Suddenly I wanted my auntie Maggie more than anything else in the world. I stayed put, my ever faithful thumb in my mouth and an arm wound round the neck of one of the grey-hounds.

Great-aunt Dodie turned and, seeing my anxiety, retraced her steps and held out her arms to me. 'Come on, Poppet, no one is going to hurt you.'

I let go of the greyhound, spat out my thumb and wound both arms around her neck as she carried me into the house.

'Meet my godchild, Rosa. Can we find her some milk and a biscuit, Esther? I'll explain in a minute.' She set me down on the hall rug and took my hand.

'Of course. Wait in the drawing room and I'll see what I can find. Would you like something, tea perhaps?' the little old woman asked.

'That would be most welcome, Esther. We'll just have a look around. I want Rosa to see my old room and the nursery. I'm sure she'll like old Dobbin. Perhaps you could bring the refreshments up there?'

Esther smiled and disappeared towards the back of the house, and Great-aunt Dodie and I made our way to a wide, carved, wooden staircase. It was on the staircase that I saw the picture of the house with the wisteria in full bloom. I had gathered a bit more courage by that point and whispered an enquiry as to where the flowers were now.

'I'm sorry, Rosa, but we've missed them. They

appear earlier in the summer, I'm afraid. Perhaps you'll see them another time. Here we are.' We stopped at a white, panelled door on the first floor. She looked around carefully and bent down and whispered in my ear, 'If I tell you a secret, can you keep it?' I nodded solemnly, and she grinned. 'Good girl,' she said and flung open the door on to one of the most beautiful rooms I have ever seen, before or since.

'This was your mother's room when *she* was a little girl, and before that it was mine. But you must not mention your mother while we are here. Do you understand? It is to be our secret until we leave. Of course, you may tell your auntie Maggie and uncle Bert about our visit – one would not want you to keep secrets from them – but just for the time being, while we're here, it is our secret. Except for Esther, and she'll keep it to herself.' Great-aunt Dodie stuck out an enormous hand and I shook it gravely.

23

The Perfumed Lady's old room was in fact two. First there was her bedroom which looked out on to the front of the house. Our windows at home tended to be on the small side, except the cafe windows of course, and this meant that our rooms were rarely blazing with sunlight the way this one was. Sometimes the old currant bun did manage to find just the spot between two rooftops that was in a direct line with one of our windows, but not for long. I was not used to the feeling of space and light and air that was my first impression when Great-aunt Dodie flung open the door. Then there was the colour scheme. I loved it on sight and it remains my favourite to this day. The walls were a rich cream and the furnishings, rugs and curtains were combinations of cream, a warm pink and apple green. The bedspread and the curtains matched exactly, something I'd never seen before. I'm not sure why I was so taken with it – it all sounds very ordinary now – but it was something to do with the mixture of sunlight, the lovely colours and the perfect proportions of the room.

Then there was the decorative plasterwork. We had some at home but nothing as complicated or as beautiful as this. The central rose around the light fitting looked like something from a wedding cake. There were roses and small birds enmeshed in a complicated tracery of foliage. If it had been my room, I'd have spent hours just gazing at that, I think. The cornices, on the other hand, had a beautiful simplicity that acted as a frame for the central glory. There were pictures on the walls. One was of a lovely cottage garden with a path winding towards a greenhouse. A robin was perched on the handle of a fork that had been left in one of the flower beds. Another showed a fairy-like being with a pipe in his mouth and he ws surrounded by small wild creatures. Birds perched everywhere, including on the end of his pipe, and squirrels, foxes, badgers, rabbits and hedgehogs cavorted around him, as if enchanted by the silent music.

I was dragged from my daydream by the sound of

Esther coming into the room bearing a tray laden with milk and biscuits for me and a pot of tea for Great-aunt Dodie.

'Let's take it into the nursery, Esther. There will be a spare cup in there and perhaps you would care to join me in some tea while we have a jolly good chat?'

Esther grinned and carefully placed the tray on the dressing table for a moment. She fished about for a second and whisked a cup out of one spacious pocket and a saucer out of the other. She placed them beside an identical set already on the tray.

'Funny you should mention that, Miss Dodie, but I took the liberty of anticipating you.'

My great-aunt threw back her white head and let out a loud hoot of laughter. 'Good old Esther, you always could read my mind, even when I was a gal and you were the tweenie. Some Eastern fellows would say we must have been sisters or some such in a previous life and I would not be surprised at that.'

She grabbed the tray and made her way to a door opposite the one we'd come in by. 'Rosa dear, could you do the honours and open the door for me? There's a good girl. Now, what do you think of that?'

I knew exactly what she was referring to as my eyes were already glued to the rocking horse that stood in front of the window. It was a dappled grey with a silky mane and tail and a lovely scarlet bridle and saddle. It was just like the one the Perfumed Lady had sent for my doll's house, only much bigger.

'Have a go if you want to, Rosa, while Esther and I exchange news. When and if you get bored with that, there are plenty more toys for you to have a look at.'

Pretty soon I was rocking fit to bust and Great-aunt Dodie and Esther were chatting about someone called 'Mr Charles'. It seemed he was no nearer getting married and was displaying a certain fecklessness that worried Esther, but Great-aunt Dodie kept on about something called 'wild oats' and having to sow them. I couldn't make head nor tail of it myself and anyway the rocking was beginning to hypnotize me. I didn't come back to myself until I heard my mother's name. It was Esther who was speaking.

'And have you heard any news of Miss Cassandra, Miss Dodie? I know Mr Charles worries about her in his own way.'

'Well, actually, Esther, that is what I wished to

talk to you about. But first, you must swear to keep anything I tell you a secret.'

Esther sounded huffy. 'You know you can trust me, Miss Dodie. I have never breathed a word to anyone about you and Mr Herbert and how long has that been going on, may I ask? Thirty years to my knowledge. How *is* Mr Herbert, by the way? Well, I hope?'

'Fine, thank you, Esther. Of course you can keep a secret. Silly of me, and I apologize. It is just that I have a feeling someone other than myself should know about this. One day we may need a witness and it is possible that I shall not be in the position to do much myself.'

'Now don't you go talking like that, Miss Dodie. By rights I should be laid to rest *years* before you.'

'Let us not get morbid, Esther. What I wanted to tell you is that Rosa here is my godchild, as I've already mentioned, but what I did not tell you is that Cassandra is her mother. Which makes Mr Charles her uncle.'

Esther did not bat an eyelid at this news. 'I thought as much as soon as I laid eyes on her,' she muttered. 'She has the look of Miss Cassandra. It's the eyes and that chin. But why are you telling *me*, Miss Dodie?'

'It is possible, Esther, that there may come a day when it is important that you were told this *now*, in cold blood as it were. She could be Charles's only heir, for example, if everyone else dies and he has no issue. Things could get heated. Accusations and denials may be flying about in all directions – you know what those cousins are. They've been itching to get a toe in the door for years. One would hate to think they would manage it by default. It never does to be too sloppy about these things.'

'Can the . . . er . . . illegitimate line inherit, Miss Dodie? I didn't think that it could.'

'I am no lawyer, Esther, but I think in certain circumstances it can. But whatever the law is now, it may be important later on to have a witness who has nothing to gain and nothing to lose. I should like you to be that witness.'

She went on to suggest that she and Esther should discuss this next door while I had a good play. Of course, Great-aunt Dodie had not had a lot to do with children and didn't realize what nosy little so-and-sos they can be. I learned a lot that afternoon. First, I found out that Charlie Fluck had nicked a letter the Perfumed Lady had written to Great-aunt Dodie. He took it out of her handbag when she wasn't looking and that was why he had come sniffing around the cafe.

'Fluck would have shown the letter to that ghastly creature Godfrey, you may be sure of that, and I expect that it was he who sent the wretched little man to check up on Cassandra in London.' Great-aunt Dodie's voice boomed loud and clear through the closed door.

Esther's voice, on the other hand, was almost too soft to hear. 'But why would he want to do that, Miss Dodie? He washed his hands of Miss Cassandra the day she left and ordered everyone else to do the same, even her own mother. I would have thought the child would have made him even more determined to get rid of her – you know how people are about unmarried mothers. They don't want their friends to know. I'd've thought he'd have let sleeping dogs lie good and quiet myself.'

'That'd be true of most people, but not of Godfrey. The possibility that Cassandra has a child would be too good an opportunity for him to miss. That man could hide behind a corkscrew he's so twisted. He's wanted sole control of Loveday Engineering for years, ever since poor Percy died and he married that vapid half-wit Evelyn. So far we've managed to keep the blighter in check between us, but if he can think of a way to use Rosa for his own ends then he will, take my word for it. We've got to keep him and his lackeys away from her and her family. They're good people, Esther. Far too good to be interfered with by the likes of Godfrey. The trouble is, poor Rosa could prove to be a very useful bargaining chip.'

I heard someone get to her feet and head towards the door that had my great lug pressed up against it. I only just got back to Dobbin in time, my heart hammering and my brains scrambled. What had chips got to do with anything? As you know, I'm very partial to chips but I had a feeling that 'bargaining' chips were something entirely different and not at all nice, and I certainly didn't fancy being one. It was all very confusing and more than a little frightening. At that moment I wanted my auntie Maggie and uncle Bert very badly indeed.

I must have looked stricken because when Great-aunt Dodie came in she asked if anything was the matter.

'Who is Godfrey and why would he want to turn me into chips?' I blurted, not caring at all that the question showed I'd been earwigging.

My great-aunt obviously decided some explanations were necessary. That's how I discovered that she had not long known about me, which is why we hadn't met up before. At least, she'd known I was expected but had thought that either my mother had had me adopted or that the pregnancy had been a false alarm and there was no baby. She had been in Delhi when I was born and when she got back there was no sign of me. It was only when I met Mr Herbert that she found out I really did exist, and she'd been angling to meet me ever since.

Far more interesting, though, was that I found out that my mum's dad, Percy, had been Great-aunt Dodie's younger brother. He'd been married to Evelyn, my grandmother, and they had had two children, Charles and Cassandra. Then Percy had died and Evelyn had married 'that ghastly Godfrey' almost before my grandfather was cold, according to Great-aunt Dodie. Evelyn and my mum and my uncle Charles had had to move out of the house when she married again and Great-aunt Dodie had cared for it until Uncle Charles had come of age, just before I was born.

By the time she'd finished telling me this potted version of the family history, I was still thoroughly confused but soothed considerably. She then suggested that we pop into the stables for a look at the horses. It was only when I was getting a handful of soft muzzle and nostrils full of essence of warm horse that I realized I'd never found out what a bargaining chip was and how I could become one. Somehow Great-aunt Dodie managed to keep dodging that question, and in the end I gave up asking it and enjoyed the horses instead.

I shall never forget the stables because that was the very first time I ever sat on a proper horse's back. Soon I was hooked. We spent a happy hour plodding around a field with me on Sadie's back and Great-aunt Dodie leading me. She said I was a natural and already had a good 'seat', whatever that was. She told me that I had inherited it from her and she was as pleased as Punch.

The journey back to Weston-super-Mare was fast and uneventful. Great-aunt Dodie was thoughtful and I was both thoughtful and knackered. It had been a long day with lots of new information and experiences to sort out in my mind.

When we were back at Dunroamin, I told everyone about Dobbin and Sadie but kept quiet about Esther, all the new relatives and the big posh house. I saved all that until I was safely tucked in bed with my beloved auntie Maggie sitting beside me. Then I told her everything, although she seemed to know most of it already. By the time she'd finished reassuring me, I was able to settle down to sleep safe in the knowledge that my real family were all around me.

24

Great-aunt Dodie and Mr Herbert were still in
residence when I woke up on the Saturday morning.
We were due to leave Aggie on Horseback on
Sunday so that we would be ready to open the
cafe bright and early on Monday morning. No one
wanted to break up the party before we had to,
especially as everyone had taken to my great-aunt
and Mr Herbert in a big way. Mr Herbert had
become Archie to all, except me that is. He
had asked me to call him 'Uncle Archie' but it didn't
seem right somehow, and anyway I was up to my
eyebrows in new relatives and wasn't about to add
yet another uncle, real or otherwise.

I was still trying to work out the relationships
between me and Mr Charles, that vapid half-wit
Evelyn, poor Percy, the revolting cousins and the

ghastly Godfrey. Auntie Maggie had explained it all to me in bed the night before, but I was still having trouble sorting them out in my mind. It's not easy to have a whole new ready-made family foisted on you out of the clear blue, and even worse if you have absolutely no idea what any of them look like. I was heartily relieved to be back in the bosom of my real family and was quite looking forward to going home. I'd miss Daisy, Hazel, Midge, Madge, Smudge and Budge of course, and Auntie Flo and Uncle Sid, but I was aching for the cafe, Luigi, Mamma and Papa Campanini, Mrs Wong and all. I was particularly looking forward to seeing our battered old Tom again.

Everyone had been busy while Great-aunt Dodie and I had been gallivanting around the countryside the day before. Mr Herbert had been hunting books in second-hand bookshops and had made one or two new acquaintances, and Auntie Maggie and Uncle Bert had been out and about with Auntie Flo and Uncle Sid and had enjoyed meeting Uncle Sid's cousin 'from Blagdon way'. Auntie Maggie was full of what a nice bloke Uncle Sid was and how lucky her Flo had been the second time around. They were almost as impressed with Uncle Sid's cousin and concluded that it must run in the family.

Madame Zelda and Paulette had spent a happy day haunting junk shops and Paulette had managed to find some additions for her famous jungle. Madame Zelda pretended to be exasperated with her. She said that pretty soon she'd be sleeping on the window ledge because there'd be no room for her, but she was smiling.

We all agreed that our holiday had been a resounding success. Auntie Flo and Uncle Sid said they'd been delighted to have us all and that we would have to come again, but in the low season, whenever that was. The sea air, sunshine and wide open spaces had put roses in all our cheeks and freckles on some of our noses, chiefly mine, although Paulette had some too.

Talking of Paulette, she positively glowed with happiness and health. She had gone from strength to strength since she had left Dave – or rather since she'd given Dave the giant elbow. She'd always had a sort of pinched, frightened look before, but now she was a different person. She had allowed her hair to return to its normal brown and she no longer tottered around on heels so high there was a serious risk of broken ankles. Gone were the tight tops with the neckline around her knees somewhere. Her new look made her seem much younger. Auntie Maggie and Auntie Flo agreed that it was a jolly good thing, and that it was about time she was allowed to be a girl again.

'She was made to grow up too fast, if you ask me, Flo,' I overheard Auntie Maggie say. 'Seems to me she never was a kid. Her mother buggered off with a GI, you know.'

'What d'you mean she buggered off with a GI? Was she one of them GI brides? Wouldn't the Yanks have 'em both or what?'

'All I know is that Paulette had just started work at Woolworth's and the poor little sod came home one day and found they'd left a note saying they'd gone to South Dakota, wherever the hell that is, and she could keep the flat if she liked. Big of 'em. Didn't even leave her a few bob. She was only fifteen and not even earning enough to pay the rent, let alone eat and everything.'

Auntie Flo clucked and shook her head sympathetically. 'Don't tell me – the landlord slung her out and she headed up West. It's the old, old story, innit?'

'You got it in one, Flo. That's how that Dave got his mitts on her. Picked her up at the station, offered her a bed for a night and had her whoring within the month. Gawd, he's a bastard, that one. How many times have we seen it? I bet the poor, grateful little cow was just going to do it the once to pay off his gambling debts. He never even bothers to change the story.'

'Madame Zelda's got a new spring in her step and all. What brought that on? She looks ten years younger!'

'She's been helping Paulette get on her feet since Dave left. They're sharing a flat now and it seems to suit 'em both and good luck to 'em is all I can say. It's nice to see Zelda happy. She's been a good friend to me, Flo, she really has. It would have been a bloody sight worse without her when you left, I can tell you.'

'Mum always said that you couldn't beat a good woman friend and that everyone should have at least one. Do you remember that she always said there was two kinds of women? Men's women and women's women and if you knew what was good for you, you'd be a woman's woman and you'd never be lonely. Said it was like belonging to a bloody great club. She wasn't wrong, neither.'

Auntie Maggie nodded sagely. 'You're right, Flo. I reckon that's at least part of the trouble with our Cassie. She has no women friends, apart from me, that is, and I'm more like a mum than a friend. It was really Bert she palled up with.'

227

As I listened to my beloved aunts I didn't understand that I was learning a valuable lesson about life and the living of it, but I was. Instead, I realized that I had spent far too much time earwigging conversations that didn't concern me. There was sunshine and donkeys to be enjoyed outdoors and it was my very last day in Aggie, so I decided that I'd better wring every last drop of enjoyment out of it. And I did.

25

Everyone was up bright and early the next morning. I was beside myself with excitement. Going away is all very well, lovely in its way, but heading home was even better. I wanted to get back to my friends, my toys, our Tom and familiarity. My new friend, Penny, had left the week before which meant I had to wait for a free grown-up to take me to say goodbye to Harry and his mob. In the end Great-aunt Dodie volunteered and Paulette came too. I was very sad to say goodbye to Hazel and friends, but Harry assured me that I could come down and visit them any time. I was a very subdued small person on my way back to Dunroamin. Paulette thought I was blubbing but I wasn't – it was just a bit of sand in my eyes. I could have sworn that Hazel had sand in her eyes too when I gave her a parting nuzzle.

Once back at Auntie Flo's though, my excitement at the thought of seeing Luigi and everyone began to mount again. I kept getting under people's feet and in the end Great-aunt Dodie offered to drive me to Bath. This would get me out of the way and I could join the train there. Auntie Maggie heaved a sigh of relief, and it was agreed that Mr Herbert could come too. He was returning to his bookshop and had elected to travel with the rest of us.

It was a lovely drive to Bath. Mr Herbert sat in the front and I had a funny little seat at the back. We whizzed past the countryside and at a place called Rickford we saw the most amazing birds foraging in a field beside some woods. They were gorgeous and had red faces, glossy green heads and long pointed tails. I let out such a yell when I saw them that Great-aunt Dodie screeched to a halt, thinking that I had fallen out of the car. Mr Herbert explained that they were cock pheasants and that the mottled brown birds with them were the females. It was hard to believe that both sorts were pheasants, but Great-aunt Dodie agreed with Mr Herbert so it must have been true. She also told me that some people shot them, hung them up in the larder until they were crawling with maggots and then cooked and ate them. I'll say this for Great-aunt Dodie, she knew how to supply interesting though often revolting details. I tucked the information away so that I could pass it on to Paulette, who was rapidly turning into my very own bird expert.

I had never seen anywhere like Bath before. The houses were made of this lovely biscuity-coloured stone and some were very grand. Great-aunt Dodie lived in a place called Lansdown Crescent that was up a steep hill. All the houses were joined together in what Mr Herbert called a terrace and Great-aunt Dodie called a crescent. I was a bit confused by this, but it turned out that both were right – it was a terrace *and* a crescent.

Great-aunt Dodie drew to a halt outside a house somewhere near the end of the elegant curve, pointed to a large, gleaming car further along the road and swore.

'Dammit, Archie, that's Ghastly Godfrey's Rolls. What the hell is *he* doing here? Dear God, I hope that creature Clunt, his shifty chauffeur, isn't with him.'

'It isn't Clunt, Aunt Dodie, it's Fluck,' I piped up helpfully.

'What? Oh yes, Fluck. We'd better get you out of here, Rosa, and post bloody haste at that. I hope to high heaven that he hasn't seen you. The little bastard may put two and two together and come up with four.' Swiftly, she swung the car round until we were heading back the way we had come.

Mr Herbert craned his neck, trying to see if there was a chauffeur in the other car. I followed his example just in time to see Charlie Fluck climb out of the driver's seat and look towards our retreating bumper, scratching his head. I tried to duck down. I didn't know exactly what the problem was, but I knew it was something to do with the bargaining chip business and keeping me a secret from Charlie Fluck and Ghastly Godfrey.

Once out on to the hill, Great-aunt Dodie put her foot down, yelling, 'Hang on!' as she did so. We shot up what remained of the slope like a bat out of hell. At the top of the hill the road sort of split; there was a bend to the right of a church and another road in front of it, going to the left. We took the left-hand turn on two wheels, I swear, with a very satisfying squeal of tyres. As we turned, I caught a glimpse of the Rolls's nose just peeping out from the crescent.

'He's coming,' I screamed above the roar of our engine and Great-aunt Dodie shoved her foot down so hard it's a wonder it didn't go through the floor.

We sped past large detached houses, trees and green verges so that they became a blur. At the brow of the hill, a long, straight stretch of road was laid out before us and our little car almost took off as it belted along it. We passed a strange-looking tower on our left, followed by some fields. Then there was a blur of cottages on our right with a pub and a racecourse opposite.

I looked behind. In the distance the distinctive outline of the Rolls could just be seen. I looked ahead in time to see another weird tower, this time on our right, and then we hit the bend. There was a road to the right of the bend which Great-aunt Dodie ignored.

'With any luck, Clunt will think we've gone down there,' she yelled above the roar of the engine. We were heading downhill when suddenly, with no warning, Great-aunt Dodie yanked the steering wheel to the left and we dived down a lane between high hedges. At last she slowed down. 'That should shake him off our tail. I just hope the little bastard doesn't think to watch the railway station. What time's the train, Archie?'

Mr Herbert seemed to be having trouble catching his breath. 'Three thirty or just before. It is one o'clock now,' he answered finally.

'Righto. Let's get back to Bath on the other road and get a spot of lunch at the house. Can't think on an empty tank now, can we? I can find out from Filkins what that sewer Godfrey wanted while I'm at it.'

The drive back to Bath was much slower and quieter. Great-aunt Dodie and Mr Herbert didn't speak much and I just sat in the back and worried. I tried to concentrate on the view but even the horses in the fields couldn't take my mind off things.

It was tricky getting through the streets of Bath unnoticed, judging by the shouts and honks of greeting aimed at us as we passed. I couldn't see anything much except fluffy clouds and rooftops on account of deciding to lie down on the back seat as we got to the outskirts of town. My great-aunt was obviously as well known in her manor as we were in ours. At last, to the relief of my bladder and my stomach, we arrived in what my aunt called 'the mews' behind Lansdown Crescent where we parked the car.

Inside the house we were confronted by a formidable old gentleman called Filkins who looked a lot less scary once Great-aunt Dodie was bossing him about.

'Ah, Filkins. Good man. Show this child to the facilities and tell Mrs Filkins that we'll take luncheon in the dining room. Perhaps you'll show the child the way back to us when she's ready?'

With a 'Yes, madam,' he whisked me away to the kitchen first and handed me over to a pale woman I took to be Mrs Filkins. She showed me where the toilet was and instructed me to be sure to wash my hands after. That done, I was handed back to Filkins who escorted me to a large sunny dining room with a high ceiling, big windows and loads of pictures on the walls. I watched as he laid three places in lonely isolation at one end of a gigantic table. Filkins didn't so much bustle as glide between table and sideboard until there were three place mats, plates, soup bowls, knives, forks, spoons and glasses twinkling in the sunshine. When he'd finished, he made towards the door, announcing that he would bring the soup directly, which left me wondering how else he was planning to bring it – via Piccadilly Circus? Before I could ask, Great-aunt Dodie was telling him to wait a moment as she wanted to ask about Mr Godfrey's visit.

'He was selling tickets, madam, to this year's Charity Ball at the Guildhall. I took the liberty of committing you to your usual ten. Mr Godfrey said a cheque at the end of the month would be satisfactory. I hope I did the right thing, madam?'

'Yes, yes, Filkins, of course you did. But what else did he say? Anything?'

'He asked who the child was, madam, but as I knew nothing about any child I was unable to enlighten him. It was only when his man Fluck hammered on the door and demanded to speak to Mr Godfrey that I learned you were back in Bath. I took the liberty of instructing Mrs Filkins to prepare luncheon as I felt sure you would return once you'd successfully eluded Mr Godfrey. May I fetch the soup now, madam? Mrs Filkins will be anxious about it getting cold.'

For one awful moment I thought my great-aunt was going to delay Filkins again. I must have looked stricken because Mr Herbert suggested she ask questions while we ate. I could've kissed him! I'm as nosy as the next bugger, as you know, but hunger had driven everything, even my growing fear of Ghastly Godfrey, almost to the back of my mind.

Just then a telephone rang and Filkins glided out to answer it. We could hear him clearly through the open door. 'Miss Loveday-Smythe's residence. Good afternoon, Mr Godfrey. A moment please.' Filkins's grey head appeared around the door, eyebrows raised in enquiry. Great-aunt Dodie nodded and began to get to her feet. The grey head disappeared.

'Yes, Madam is on her way to the telephone now,

Mr Godfrey. Will you wait just a moment? No, Mr Godfrey, I still know nothing about a child. Perhaps you should address that question to Miss Loveday-Smythe, who may be better able to answer it.'

On hearing this, my great-aunt mouthed, 'Oh, well done, Filkins!' and beamed her approval. She disappeared into the hallway and Mr Herbert and I heard her booming, 'Make it snappy, Godfrey, my soup's getting cold.'

There was silence for a few moments, apart from some heavy breathing that became heavier until it sounded how I imagined a wounded bull would sound. Then there was an explosion of indignation. 'I am not in the habit of ferrying children about, Godfrey, as you well know – not since my nephew grew up and you drove my niece away!'

More silence and more wounded bulls followed, a whole herd of 'em. The next explosion made me want to look for blood on the carpet; Mr Herbert ducked, and we weren't even in the same room.

'Cassandra's private life is no longer any concern of yours or her mother's, Godfrey. I'm sure that had she wished to confide in you, she would have. As you will know from reading my correspondence, her daughter was fostered. That is all I know on the subject.

'No, I have no idea what you are talking about, unless your man somehow managed to mistake my friend, Archie Herbert, for a child. Has he been drinking? I shouldn't be surprised – Fluck's an unpleasant, shifty-looking character who riffles through handbags and steals letters.' There was another longish pause, then she was off again. 'If I choose to take off on a jaunt around the countryside in the motor in preference to receiving you in my home, that is entirely my own concern, Godfrey. If you simply must know, I find you to be rather an oily specimen and have always striven to avoid your company. Now my soup will wait no longer. Good day to you.'

We heard a crash and Great-aunt Dodie came back into the room, looking very red in the face, closely followed by Filkins with a tray bearing a large bowl with a lid called a tureen. I didn't know whether to faint with relief at the sight of food, or with fear at the sight of my relative's kisser. Once again, I understood why Afghan tribesmen took to the hills when she got a strop on; it was something to do with the glitter in those periwinkle-blue eyes.

We never had soup in the summer at the cafe, and as I slurped my way through the brown Windsor I knew why; hot soup and hot days don't really go together. I felt better about the cold game pie and lettuce, tomato and radish salad that followed, but to be frank I wasn't up to giving the food much attention other than shovelling it into my grateful gob. This was because I was too busy listening in to the conversation between Great-aunt Dodie and Mr Herbert. They seemed to have completely forgotten I was there.

'It's no good, Archie, I know that creature Godfrey is up to something. He was trying to get me to give him chapter and verse on young Rosa and he didn't even trouble to hide the fact that Clunt stole Cassandra's letter. The man's without shame. I'd look a fool reporting the theft of a letter and there is precious little else I can do about it and the sewer knows it. Whatever happens we must not allow young Rosa here to fall into that man's clutches!'

Great-aunt Dodie's tone was grim and her hawk nose looked sharper and more dangerous than ever. I felt very frightened and I desperately wanted my auntie Maggie and uncle Bert, even though I was convinced that this formidable-looking woman would defend me to the death if need be. The trouble was, although I knew *who* was threatening my world, I didn't really understand *why*.

Mr Herbert was all for us getting our food down

in a hurry and making a rapid exit. 'I think it's best, Dodie dear. Then we can hole up quietly somewhere in case Godfrey returns here. It might be wise to warn Filkins to continue to deny any knowledge of Rosa and to insist that no child has been here today, just to keep the waters muddy.

'I also advise leaving by taxi. Your car is too distinctive and you're far too well known. Perhaps you should ask Filkins to telephone your usual man to see if he can oblige us.'

It was agreed, and we bolted the rest of our dinner. I couldn't even tell you what we had for afters, I was in such a state. Within half an hour we were driving through the Bath streets on our way to the station. We stopped only once, while Mr Herbert nipped into a newsagent's and returned with *The Times* and *Schoolfriend* and *Girl* for me. Personally, I preferred the *Eagle* or the *Topper* but I didn't like to complain. It was nice of him to think of me at all. I'm jolly glad he did, though, because we had more than an hour before the train and reading would stop me worrying and longing for Auntie Maggie.

When we stopped again, I was bustled into the Station Hotel by Great-aunt Dodie while Mr Herbert settled up with the cabbie. I tried hard to read my comics while we had afternoon tea – cream, scones, everything – but I wasn't really hungry and my attention kept straying to the grown-ups' conversation.

Mr Herbert said there was no reason for Ghastly Godfrey to think we'd head for the station; for all he knew, Fluck had been mistaken or I was simply down for a little holiday and there was no saying when I'd leave again. 'If, on the other hand, he's being extra watchful, he might just think to check the station. If he shows up, we can always catch a later train; inconvenient, but not impossible.'

In the end, we decided that Great-aunt Dodie would 'do a recce' just before the train was due. If she spotted Godfrey or Charlie Fluck she'd signal, and Mr Herbert and I would carry on lying low in the hotel. If the way was clear, she'd give another signal and we'd make a dash for the train.

A fair old discussion took place before we decided what signals my great-aunt should use. We finally settled on blowing her nose a couple of times on her large white linen hanky if there was trouble, and waving if there wasn't. The nose-blowing was my idea. Actually, I suggested she could rootle about a bit as if she was looking for one of those horrible sharp bogies that dig into the inside of your nostril, but she and Mr Herbert thought nose-blowing would be better. Auntie Maggie was always telling me that nice girls didn't pick their noses, especially in public, and I expect Great-aunt Dodie thought the same. Once that was decided there was nothing to do but carry on waiting. I fidgeted and squirmed in an agony of impatience.

Finally, the time came for my great-aunt to leave the hotel. Mr Herbert and I took up our positions at the window so that we had a good view. She must have done several careful laps of the station platforms, ticket office and forecourt because we kept seeing her flitting across our line of vision. At last there she was again, firmly planted so that we could see her frantically waving her hanky.

Mr Herbert and I made a dash for it – just like those spies crossing no-man's-land in the war films – and arrived, panting, just as the train pulled into the platform. It was a miracle of timing. We saw Uncle Bert's beloved bonce sticking out of a window towards the front of the train, and Great-aunt Dodie yanked me clear off my feet and pounded up the platform with me in her arms. Poor Mr Herbert was left to puff along behind us with our luggage. When we were at the right carriage, I was dumped unceremoniously on the platform as she yanked open the door and then almost threw me inside, much to the astonishment of my loved ones.

'She ain't been a little toe-rag, has she, so that you can't wait to be shot of her?' my auntie Maggie demanded, shooting me a stern you-wait-'til-I-tell-you-your-fortune look.

She relaxed slightly when Great-aunt Dodie assured her that I had been an absolute poppet, and that Archie would explain and she'd see us very soon. As she said that, Mr Herbert arrived, and she bundled him into the carriage too as if he was a large sack of potatoes.

She'd just slammed the door behind him when the whistle blew and we were off. I was about to wave goodbye when I caught a glimpse of Charlie Fluck's head, complete with chauffeur's cap, behind her. I made for the safety of Auntie Maggie's lap toot sweet and kept my head buried in her large, comforting bosom while Mr Herbert explained all.

I hadn't realized just how frightened I had been until I was swathed in the reassuring smells of warm Auntie Maggie and Uncle Bert's pipe.

26

The only things I remember about the train journey from Bath to London were lots of talk, Auntie Maggie's lap, the comforting sounds and smells of my loved ones and Uncle Bert finding a gobstopper in my ear. I was busy slurping this and staring out of the window when I must have fallen asleep. What's more, I must have stayed asleep for ages because I barely remember arriving at Paddington, being bundled into a cab and finally arriving back at the cafe. That brought me round. The sheer joy of being back in familiar surroundings, with friends on all sides, made me feel safe again. All I had seen and heard in Bath had made me very nervous and what I wanted most was to get back to normal. I was even beginning to miss school and look forward to the new term.

Mamma Campanini had prepared a meal for us and we went to her place to eat it. Even Mr Herbert came. I got the feeling that he quite liked being around us and we certainly liked having him. He'd sort of slotted in and you couldn't see the seam.

While we were at Mamma Campanini's, Uncle Bert filled Luigi and the others in on what had been happening. There was a general murmur of unease at the news that Charlie Fluck had seen me with my great-aunt and it was agreed that everyone would keep an eye open for Charlie or any other suspicious person. Quite suddenly Uncle Bert began to laugh.

Auntie Maggie was indignant. 'What's so funny, may I ask?'

'I was just wondering, Maggie, how the hell we're supposed to pick out a suspicious person round here? *Everyone*'s bleeding suspicious!'

'Well, you talk for yourself, Bert Featherby. There ain't nothing suspicious about *me*. P'raps you had better tell us what this Godfrey person looks like, Mr Herbert? It might be a help.'

Mr Herbert did his best to oblige, describing Ghastly Godfrey in some detail. The trouble was, he sounded like a million other blokes, only better dressed. According to Mr Herbert he was shortish, about five foot seven, with slicked-back dark brown hair going grey at the temples and he wore spectacles. Apparently, the most striking thing about him was his skin; it had a yellowish tinge from years in the tropics.

Meanwhile we decided to put the word out for my mum to present herself as soon as humanly possible. She was back from Paris, and had been seen in a Mayfair gambling club with a Greek ship owner who was losing heavily at the roulette table.

Once I'd eaten, I got all dopey again and I was tucked up on Mamma Campanini's bed while the rest made a night of it. It seems to me, looking back, that my lot were always having get-togethers of one sort or another. Some were full-blown parties but mostly they were just small, convivial gatherings – what Auntie Maggie called a 'muffin worry' and Uncle Bert a 'bunfight'. Telly hadn't really got a grip in those days and people still sang around the joanna on a Sunday after dinner or tea. We went to the pictures a lot, too, and played card games like Snap, Whist, Fish, Rummy, Beat Your Neighbour Out of Doors and Happy Families in the evenings while we listened to the radio. Now I like the telly as much as the next person, but I sometimes miss the days when people did things together.

I dimly remember being carried out of the

Campaninis' place by Uncle Bert. It was dark – well, at least as dark as it ever gets with street lamps and the neon. I woke the next morning in my own bed with the light streaming in through my thin summer curtains. Tom had honoured me with his presence some time during the night because I could feel his large, soft body throbbing gently against my legs. I opened my eyes and gave his tattered, lace-curtain lugs a loving fumble. It was good to be home.

Monday morning followed the usual routine. I turned the closed sign to open and Uncle Bert shot the bolts on the cafe door. A constant stream of seedy-looking strangers ordered coffees and teas and nursed their hangovers. Most of them kept looking at the clock, anxious to get to work on time. The rush would die to a trickle by about half-past eight as they hurried off to offices, shops or warehouses. There would be a bit of a lull, then the locals would wander in for a gossip and a coffee. To everyone's astonishment, the first local in that morning was Sharky Finn. It was not like Sharky to put in an appearance before noon at the earliest, so we knew it was serious.

'Bert, Maggie, a word in your shell-likes if I may. Shall we retire to the corner table? A little privacy is required, I think.'

Mrs Wong waited long enough for the three of them to get settled, then she drifted over with a Sharky special. I could smell the brandy as she walked past me. I sidled up behind her and settled myself on Uncle Bert. I don't know how I knew, but I was convinced that whatever Sharky had to say, it was about me. Everything pointed to it somehow. All that chasing around the countryside hotly pursued by the slimy Charlie Fluck; the sudden advent of hordes of unknown relatives; the ancestral home complete with loyal retainers; all these things had come into my life in the last few days. It seemed inevitable that an unprecedented visit from Sharky, in the morning no less, should have something to do with it all. And I was right.

Sharky was silent for a moment while he mumbled his dead cigar around a bit. Removing the blackened stump from his mouth, he took a swig of his coffee and began to speak. 'Bert, Maggie, I won't tart it up. Someone's broken into my office and stolen the file pertaining to Rosie's guardianship. That was all that was stolen. Is there any sign of a break-in here?'

Auntie Maggie and Uncle Bert looked at each other. Then Uncle Bert took me gently round the waist and lowered me to the ground as he stood up.

'I'll just go and check to see if our copy's still here, Sharky,' he said, and off he went.

We waited in silence until he came back a few minutes later. He looked grave. 'The bathroom window's been forced. It's not hard to get at. There's that alley and the wall. You could easily reach the bathroom window from that wall, no trouble at all. Done it meself when I was locked out. Professional search though. No mess, but they found our copy and it's gone.'

I just caught a stricken look that passed from Auntie Maggie to Uncle Bert when Sharky held up a hand. He leaned forward. 'Just as well I took the precaution of sending the third copy to my safe place then, isn't it?' he said in a voice I could barely hear. 'The point is, who took it and, what's more important, why? I have a feeling that if we can answer the first question, the second will answer itself.'

'I think we had better go upstairs, Sharky,' Uncle Bert decided. 'There's a lot to tell you. Maggie love, do you think you can hold the fort? I'll try to be as quick as I can. Tell the punters they'll have to wait if they want something fancy.'

I don't know what Uncle Bert and Sharky talked about upstairs because I wasn't invited to join them.

But when they came down, they both looked serious. Sharky left, muttering something about checking a few things out and getting back to Uncle Bert when he had some answers. Then Auntie Maggie and Uncle Bert went into a huddle and Auntie Maggie kept looking over at me with a troubled expression. I was trying to eat my breakfast, but it was hard to get the toast past the lump in my throat.

I knew that my grown-ups were afraid, so I was afraid too.

27

I crept around for the next few days, trying to keep out of sight. I found I kept staring out of the windows at the street or the alleyway, and once I caught both Auntie Maggie and Uncle Bert at it too. There was an uneasy feeling about the place, rather like the feeling that ran through the area when a gang war was brewing or the police decided to crack down on gambling or the working girls. Everyone was jumpy.

It didn't take long for the word to spread that Sharky's office and our flat had had an unwelcome visitor some time on Sunday. Various theories were put forward as to who was responsible, but *we* knew that Charlie Fluck and very possibly Ghastly Godfrey were behind it. What we could not understand was how Charlie had managed to get to London before we did.

Luigi was practical. 'Simple, innit? He didn't do it himself. He got someone on the blower who did it for him.'

Of course! It was obvious when you thought about it. Old Mrs Roberts from the newsagent's said she'd seen Dave hanging about early on Sunday evening. He'd been standing in next door's doorway as if he was waiting. She'd thought he was planning to give Paulette a hard time about something. This was discussed at length but, as far as we were concerned, Charlie and Dave didn't know each other. Madame Zelda muttered something about 'the flea always being able to find the bleeding dog'. I was on the point of asking her who she thought the flea was and who the dog, and then realized I didn't have to, especially as Auntie Maggie and Uncle Bert agreed that Charlie and Dave did make a likely couple.

Meanwhile, the word went out even more urgently for the Perfumed Lady to present herself at the cafe, and I was sent round to Mr Herbert's with an equally urgent message for Great-aunt Dodie. He called her immediately, while I waited, and she said she'd come to London as soon as she could. She told me to tell Uncle Bert that she had seen nothing of either Godfrey or Clunt. I had my mouth open to yell 'Fluck' but snapped it shut again. What was the point? We knew who she meant. It was arranged that she would stay with Mr Herbert and that we would all meet to talk abut the thefts and try to work out what it all added up to and what we could do about it, if anything. As always, everyone kept their eyes open wide.

It was Luigi who saw Charlie first. It was late afternoon on Thursday when he came into the cafe and told us that he'd seen him disappearing into Theresa's place. She still lived above the green-grocer's on the corner of Frith Street. So Charlie was just down the road! This was a turn-up for the books. It meant that Charlie and Dave *did* know each other, or that Charlie was on visiting terms with Theresa, which probably meant that he and Dave had at least met.

Uncle Bert, Auntie Maggie and Luigi went into a huddle to discuss this latest turn of events. Luckily, Luigi had had the sense to get a couple of his young nephews, Giorgio and Luciano, to keep an eye on Theresa's as he thought that we would want to know when Charlie left and where he went. He was right, although as it happened we didn't need the spies. Not half an hour after Luigi turned up, Charlie burst through the door. I just had time to disappear behind the counter.

'All right, you lot! No more messin' about. Where's that bloody Cassandra Loveday-Smythe? I know you know her and I know you know her aunt 'cos I saw that kid wiv her only the other day. You may be able to fool Mr Godfrey but you can't pull the wool over my eyes and don't think you can.'

Uncle Bert wiped his hands on a dishcloth and took his time before he spoke. When he did, his voice was very quiet. I could barely hear him and I was crouched at his feet, behind the counter. 'Now what can we do for you, Mr Fluck? Usually, when people want information, they ask polite, like. They don't come barging in here yelling their heads off. P'raps if you adjust your manners we might feel more inclined.'

'I think, Mr Albert John bleedin' Feaverby, that you had better make up your mind to co-operate.' I peeked round the edge of the counter. Charlie was waving a large brownish envelope in the air. 'Or take the consequences, if you get my drift? Now I know who the brat belongs to, I've decided to stop pussy-footin' round you lot. There's one or two people who might be interested in what I can tell 'em. I want to see the kid's mum and I want to see her soon.'

Uncle Bert opened his mouth to speak but before he could say anything Charlie was off again. 'Or I'll just take this little lot to her family and see what they make of it.' He brandished the envelope again. 'I'll be back on Monday, round about four o'clock. Tell her to be here. Or else!' The cafe door slammed and he was gone.

Luigi, Uncle Bert and Auntie Maggie looked at each other and I crept out from my hiding place. Nobody said anything. At last Auntie Maggie roused herself and told me to nip next door and get Sharky. Uncle Bert added that perhaps I could ask Sharky to telephone Mr Herbert and ask him to get Great-aunt Dodie up to town as soon as she could make it. I had just got to the door when he added as an afterthought that perhaps Sharky could also try telephoning my mum. I galloped off to do his bidding.

Sharky was in his office with Muriel when I arrived panting at his door. The room was wreathed in cigar smoke, and several cups littered the surfaces that were not covered with piles of paper. Muriel had a notepad in one hand and a pencil poised in the other. Sharky was lying back in his chair, staring vacantly at the ceiling.

I gave my message in a rush in case I should forget any of it.

Sharky sat bolt upright, tipping a cup over as he did so. The thick black dregs of coffee dripped steadily on to the floor. 'Say again, young Rosie. Slowly this time.'

I repeated my requests and told him what Charlie had said.

'Blackmail, is it? We'll have to see about that. Muriel, get me Mr Herbert's number and Cassandra's. They're in the book. No, not the telephone book, *our* book. Then give 'em a bell. Put them through to me. Tell Bert I'll be down in a moment, will you, Rosie?'

Madame Zelda was in the cafe when I got back and it was obvious by her face that someone had told her Charlie was around. I passed on Sharky's message, then asked Madame Zelda where Paulette was.

'She's gone for a job, Rosie. They're hiring at the Lyon's Corner House at Marble Arch and she thought she'd give it a go. She should be back in a mo.'

Almost as soon as she'd spoken, the door opened and in came Paulette, looking flustered but hopeful she'd got the job. She joined Madame Zelda and caught up with all our news. By the time Sharky appeared, everyone looked worried. Mr Herbert had called Great-aunt Dodie and she had promised to arrive that evening. All we could do was wait.

When not even my doll's house could distract me, I went to play with Kathy Moon in the square for an hour or so. By the time I got home again, the cafe was closed but Madame Zelda, Paulette, Luigi and Sharky were all sitting around waiting for Mr Herbert and my great-aunt to arrive. The ashtrays on their tables were full, and cups and glasses were strewn about the place. Auntie Maggie and Uncle Bert were going through the motions of clearing the decks for the morning. I could tell that they were thinking about other things though. They looked strained and I just sort of hung around. Nobody seemed to have much to say.

At last a taxi drew up outside and Great-aunt Dodie arrived, accompanied by Mr Herbert. Uncle Bert let them in and introduced them to Luigi and Sharky, then filled in the details of the thefts and Charlie's visit.

Great-aunt Dodie's eyes glittered and she was quiet for quite a while. 'I don't think the little bastard has told Godfrey everything,' she said eventually. 'Clunt is firmly fixed on the main chance, which, from what you say, he seems to think is blackmail. Of course both he and Godfrey are desperate to find Cassandra. She's the real key to all this interest in young Rosa. I'm convinced that Godfrey means to use the child as a way of making Cassandra do what he wants.'

'And what would that be, d'you think?' Sharky's voice was thoughtful.

'It's always been his ambition to get his hands on the family business. When my brother Percy died, Godfrey, who already worked for Loveday Engineering, married Evelyn almost before the coffin was out of the house, in order to get control of her stock. She takes no interest in the business at all.' Great-aunt Dodie's voice was sharp with disapproval as it always was when she mentioned the mysterious woman who was my grandmother.

Sharky had sat up at the word 'business'. 'And what is the family business, exactly?'

'Loveday Engineering. It used to concentrate on making bits for bridges before the war but expanded into producing components for aircraft, tanks and automobiles when the hostilities created a huge demand. We churn out an astounding number and variety of ball-bearings as well, though God knows what they go into.'

Sharky was leaning forward. 'And how do you think this man Godfrey is planning to use Rosie here if he can get his hands on her?' His eyes never left my great-aunt's face.

'It's very simple, really. He will either use Rosa to pressure Cassandra into voting his way at board meetings or he might even get her to hand over her shares to him, lock, stock and barrel. It would save an awful lot of trouble. When poor Percy died he left his stock equally between Evelyn and the two children. As the children were obviously too young to look after their inheritance, Godfrey did it for them. Then they grew up.'

Everyone looked bewildered except Sharky, who nodded. 'So the trouble started when Godfrey lost effective control of the company?'

'Yes indeed. You've got it.' Great-aunt Dodie suddenly looked old and weary. 'It has been dashed awkward with Cassandra disappearing and refusing point blank to deal with Godfrey and the business. Godfrey and Charles are always at loggerheads over every decision and I often have to step in and cast my vote to decide an issue. Which puts me on the wrong side of at least one of them and sometimes both.'

'Has Cassandra been using her money since she became old enough to deal with it herself?' Sharky asked the question that was troubling everyone. If the Perfumed Lady was rich, how come she was always skint?

'To my knowledge she has never touched it. When she left the Hall, she left everything: her family, her clothes – everything. Naturally Charles makes sure that her share of the profits is banked for her, and before he was old enough I saw to it. That's one of the many reasons Godfrey and I loathe each other. I made sure that he could not get his grubby hands on either the children's money or their shares. He's a greedy bastard, Godfrey.'

I think that Auntie Maggie, Uncle Bert, Madame Zelda and Paulette may have known some of this already, because they showed no surprise. Luigi and Sharky, on the other hand, seemed taken aback.

Luigi broke the long silence. 'If she's worth a few bob, what the hell is she doing flogging herself for a bottle of gin, then?'

The question hung in the air, unanswered.

'So it has come to that, has it?' Great-aunt Dodie said in an unsteady voice. 'I have wondered. I have sent money to her when she has asked and when she has deigned to let me know where she is. Once, we met at the Dorchester for tea and I told her about her account but she merely said that she would rather die than touch anything Godfrey provided, directly or indirectly. She could not or would not understand that it was hers and had little to do with Godfrey. She just said that he ran the business that brought in the money and repeated that she would not touch it.'

I noticed that during this bit of the conversation Great-aunt Dodie's voice wobbled. Mr Herbert moved a little closer to her and took her hand under the table; Luigi kept shaking his head slightly, as if to clear it; and Sharky stared absently at my great-aunt but said nothing.

Auntie Maggie's voice was brisk. 'I'm sure Cassie has her reasons, and whatever they are, they're obviously good enough for her. But chewing this particular lump of fat isn't sorting anything out. We need to find Cassie and we need to have some sort of plan for dealing with Charlie on Monday, with or without her.'

'You're right, Maggie,' Sharky said. 'I tried calling the number I had for her, but it's out of order. Sounds as if she hasn't paid the bill. Of course, she could have moved again and not let anyone know yet. Has anyone seen her since she was with that Greek at the Sovereign Club?'

Everyone shook their head.

'Righto,' Sharky continued. 'That's our first

priority then. Find her, sober her up if necessary and have her here for Monday. I think it is unlikely that we shall find out exactly what Fluck wants unless she's here. If he felt like telling any of us, he would have done so.'

Luigi was charged with getting his numerous relatives and contacts on to the search, Madame Zelda said she'd ask her punters and Uncle Bert said we'd ask ours, although he said it was likely that we would just have to wait and see.

'It's not as if the word isn't out,' he commented. 'It's been out since we got home from Aggie. She must either have gone to ground for some reason or she's gone walkabout again. She must take after you, Dodie. She's always off gallivanting somewhere.'

'What about asking T.C. to find her?' This was Auntie Maggie's suggestion and it was met with a considerable silence. It never occurred to any of our lot to involve Old Bill in our troubles. It just wasn't done. On the other hand, everyone liked T.C. despite his calling and they knew he had a soft spot for my mum, despite hers.

'It's worth a shot, I s'pose,' Uncle Bert muttered reluctantly, and so we decided to enlist him as well.

The next item on the agenda was what to do about the break-ins, if anything. It went against everyone's grain to let Charlie and Dave get away with these. All doubt that they were involved had disappeared since Charlie's visit. He was far too sure of himself and, when he waved around the envelope that most of us assumed had contained my adoption papers, he'd more or less told us so. On the other hand, we couldn't let it go indefinitely. Sharky and Uncle Bert pointed out that if the word got around that you could break in and nick things at will, every bugger'd be at it in no time. No, retribution was essential, but after the other matter was sorted, not before.

Great-aunt Dodie, Mr Herbert, Madame Zelda and Paulette stayed on long after I had been put to bed. Luigi left straight after the meeting, saying that he had better make a start on finding the Perfumed Lady. Uncle Bert went out too as he had an appointment with Maltese Joe. Sharky hung on for another brandy or two and a quiet chat with my great-aunt. He gave me a funny look when he got up to go. At the door, he asked Auntie Maggie something in a very quiet voice. All I could hear was 'Bert' and 'tomorrow' and 'serious money', and then he was gone.

Auntie Maggie turned back to the others sitting in the corner. 'Anybody hungry?' she asked.

Great-aunt Dodie didn't want to be a bother and it took a while to persuade her that she wasn't. We all had egg, bacon, chips and fried tomatoes and it was almost as good as Uncle Bert's.

Shortly after our meal I was taken upstairs for my bath, but first I got to kiss everyone goodnight and Great-aunt Dodie promised to come and read a bit of *The Wind in the Willows* to me. I felt I needed the comfort. I always associated Ratty, Toad, Moley and Badger with the Perfumed Lady. I think, looking back, it gave me the comfort of feeling that she was somewhere near and safe. More than anything, I wanted her to be safe.

28

Friday and Saturday crawled by. Madame Zelda, Paulette and Luigi breezed in and out at regular intervals, but nobody had anything to report. The search was still on for the Perfumed Lady. Luigi had been to her flat but the woman who answered the door swore that she had never even heard of my mum.

On the Saturday, Great-aunt Dodie took me to the zoo and then for tea at a posh hotel. I liked the rides at the zoo – the elephants were almost as good as donkeys – but not hairy enough or blessed with the same sense of humour. It was a nice trip out and we got along fine together, but we were both a bit subdued. It seems, looking back, that it was always like that when we were hunting for my mum. Everyone went a bit quiet, preoccupied. It was as if we were holding our breath, afraid of what we might find.

The cafe was closed for the day when we got back. Madame Zelda and Paulette were upstairs with Auntie Maggie, and Uncle Bert was out. Auntie Maggie was sewing labels into my new school clothes. The autumn term was almost upon us, and I was glad; in fact I was even looking forward to it. I had enjoyed our stay at Aggie on Horseback, don't get me wrong, but I was relieved to be home again. I had hoped that life would settle back to normal as soon as we clapped eyes on the dear old cafe. But it hadn't. I was heartily sick of alarms and surprises. Perhaps, I thought, the routine of school would help me to forget about the new family that had been foisted on me. We had got along fine without them so far; and now I felt pretty keen to get along without them again. I was happy enough to include Great-aunt Dodie and Mr Herbert in our clan, but I really didn't want the others. Somewhere deep inside me was the conviction that had Ghastly Godfrey or the vapid half-wit Evelyn been fit to know, then the Perfumed Lady wouldn't have run away from them. But she had, and, what is more, I now knew she would rather starve than have them anywhere near her.

Great-aunt Dodie stayed long enough to have a swift whisky and then left. She and Mr Herbert were going to the theatre but she didn't say what she was planning to see. Not that it would have meant much to me if she had. Despite being surrounded by theatres, we didn't often go. We went to the pictures instead.

Paulette read *The Borrowers* to me for a bit when I was in bed that night. Rustles and squeaks from under the floorboards ceased to hold any terrors for me once I'd discovered these wonderful little people. I loved the notion of the tiny little tea-leaves nicking cotton reels, drawing pins and buttons for their own purposes. I took to making up miniature beds in matchboxes in case they fancied a lie-down and left out tempting snacks on the minute dolls' plates, and was most disappointed when the bed covers remained unruffled and the food untouched. All in all, I was so taken with *The Borrowers* that I rather hoped they'd move into my doll's house. Paulette joined in the make-believe and we had a fine old time. Uncle Bert still wasn't home when I finally went to sleep at about ten o'clock.

I was woken up two or three hours later by the sound of the cafe door being slammed and stumbling steps on the stairs. Muffled giggles and soft swear words floated up to me. I heard the bed creak next door as Auntie Maggie climbed out of it. Then I heard her open the bedroom door.

'About time and all, Bert Featherby. Where the hell have you been?'

'Shoosh, Maggie love, you'll wake our Rosie. Come and see what I've found.'

I heard two sets of footsteps descend the stairs into the cafe. It sounded as if Uncle Bert fell the last few, judging by the muttered 'Sod it!'

'Watch yourself, Bert,' Auntie Maggie hissed. 'You're Brahms, aren't you? Gordon Bennett, I'll say you are. You smell like a bleeding distillery.'

I didn't hear much after that and I must have gone back to sleep. The next thing I knew, it was morning and Auntie Maggie was standing beside my bed.

'Morning, love. I've got your breakfast almost on the table. Be as quiet as a mouse when you get up, won't you. Uncle Bert has a sore head this morning and so has your mum. So creep about until they surface, there's a good girl.'

When Uncle Bert did appear, he looked like death warmed up. His eyes were bleary, his skin red and dry-looking, his hair a mess. He couldn't even face his pipe, let alone breakfast. Auntie Maggie made him endless cups of black coffee and at last he was in a position to tell us about the night before.

He had gone out with Luigi but they had decided to split up and spread their search a little wider. Uncle Bert had toured the spielers and had finally found my mum with her Greek in tow at one of Maltese Joe's places. It had taken a while to prise her loose from her Greek, Uncle Bert told us. The Perfumed Lady had had a few, and hadn't been too keen to leave such a good meal ticket. The Greek was loaded and generous with it, a combination that my mum always found irresistible – which I reflected later, made it all the more sinister that she'd abandoned a family stiff with readies. Come the end, Maltese Joe's Frankie had had to sit on the Greek while Uncle Bert hustled my mum out of the place and into a taxi. It had been hard work getting her to the cafe – 'like wrestling with a bloody octopus', or so Uncle Bert said.

The rest of that Sunday was spent trying to sober my mum up and get her to understand what was going on. It was impossible to leave her because she kept trying to make a break for it. She had been on what Auntie Maggie called 'a bender' for some days and wasn't ready to come out of it yet, hence her bids for freedom. Auntie Maggie called in reinforcements and Madame Zelda, Paulette and Luigi all took turns in staying with her.

No one would let me see her but I kept hearing her sobs and screams. She was ranting on about snakes crawling all over her and bugs coming out of the wall. Or was it bugs crawling all over her and snakes coming out of the wall? I'm not sure, but I did know it was all very scary.

It was quite a relief when Great-aunt Dodie and Mr Herbert showed up with a large bottle of gin. The general opinion was that the snakes and bugs would disappear once she had a little drink. The trick was to keep it little.

29

The arrival of Great-aunt Dodie had an amazing effect on the Perfumed Lady.

You could tell the old lady was not amused as soon as she came in the door and heard the racket coming from my mother's room. Her awesome features hardened as Paulette explained that my mum had a dose of the 'screaming abdabs'. It was *years* before I discovered that the correct medical term for the DTs was not 'screaming abdabs'. Anyway, the old girl's countenance was set like concrete as she instructed Mr Herbert to look after me while she sorted out my mother. We heard her stump steadily up the stairs and Paulette remarked she was glad she wasn't the one in line for a bollocking. We just had time to nod our agreement with this sentiment when we heard, 'Cassandra, stop that nonsense *immediately*.'

With that, Auntie Maggie, Uncle Bert, Madame Zelda and Luigi trooped down the stairs and into the cafe. We were all very subdued as we listened to the sounds wafting down from above. It was obvious that a slug of gin had worked its miracle and the snakes and bugs had disappeared. It was also obvious that Great-aunt Dodie was not interested in explanations or excuses.

'I said be quiet, Cassandra, and get into that bath,' we heard her say. 'No, leave the door open and *I'll* hang on to your clothes. You are *not* going to make a break for it through the window. If you do, you'll have to do it starkers.'

We heard vigorous splashing noises and yelps of protest followed by a lot of muttering punctuated by my mother's voice shouting, 'I won't!'

'Oh yes, you *will*,' Great-aunt Dodie replied. 'You made this filthy mess and by God you will clear it up.' Then she roared down the stairs, 'Rosa, please bring a bucket, a mop and a floorcloth up here, will you?'

Auntie Maggie and I scurried into the kitchen to get the things and I trundled up the stairs with them toot bloody sweet, I can tell you. I shall never forget the sight that greeted me when I got to the door of my mum's room. The place was a tip. Furniture had been overturned, there was sick on the floor and all over the bed and my mum was huddled in the middle, her thin arms wrapped around her heaving body. Great-aunt Dodie towered over her, face stern as she held what looked like a cocktail dress between the finger and thumb of her right hand. Her voice was quiet but you wouldn't have wanted to argue with it.

'I said get dressed, Cassandra, and I mean it. You may have another snort when and only when this room is clean again and you have washed your bedding. The sooner you start, the sooner you may have your gin.'

Now I was something of an authority on the sulks and my mum had the right hump. Her face was sullen and her voice whiny but defiant. 'I won't! I don't feel well and if I start on that lot I'll only throw up again. I didn't ask you to come and I'm too old to be pushed around like a little kid. So piss off back to Bath and leave me alone!'

Great-aunt Dodie drew herself up to her considerable height, grabbed my mum by her thin upper arm and heaved her to her feet. Anger shone in her eyes as she leaned very close to my mum's startled, tear-stained and blotchy face. I had to strain to hear her voice, but the menacing tone was unmistakable.

'Listen carefully, as I shall say this only once. These good people have cared for you and your child for years now. They have done it willingly because they love you and they love Rosa here. They did not owe you anything but they have mopped you up, bailed you out, paid your fines and nursed you whenever the occasion has arisen. And how do you repay them? By disturbing their rest, vomiting all over their home, throwing tantrums and refusing to clear up your messes after you. But not this time, my girl, not this time. *This* time you are going to do the decent thing. You are going to clear this lot up, make yourself presentable and *be* here, sober and in full command of what passes for your wits when that repulsive little man Clunt shows up tomorrow afternoon. Do you understand me?'

My mum opened her mouth to protest.

Great-aunt Dodie tightened her grip and gave her a little shake. 'Don't argue. Not if you know what is good for you. Just allow me to tell you what will happen if you continue with this nonsense.' She let go of my mum's arm, picked up the gin and walked to the bathroom with it. My mum trailed after her, her eyes fixed greedily on the bottle.

Slowly, very slowly, Great-aunt Dodie unscrewed the cap and began tipping the contents down the toilet, talking as she did so. 'I shall keep pouring until I see you making vigorous efforts to clear up that room, then I shall stop. You may have another drink when your work is finished. Now what is it to be? Speak up, girl. Your supplies are getting more limited by the second.'

She tipped the bottle a little further and the clear, evil-smelling liquid glugged steadily panwards. My mum let out a defeated whimper and began to climb into her clothes, never taking her eyes off the gin bottle. The glugging stopped but Great-aunt Dodie didn't move away from the toilet until my mum was on her hands and knees with the floorcloth. I jumped slightly when Great-aunt Dodie spoke again.

'Rosa, would you get me a chair, dear, so I may sit as I supervise? I think you had better join the others downstairs when you have done that; Cassandra and I have some things to discuss. Could you ask your aunt or uncle to join us, please?'

I did not hang about. Auntie Maggie and Uncle Bert opted to be in on the discussions, and Paulette, Madame Zelda, Luigi, Mr Herbert and I traipsed next door to Paulette and Madame Zelda's place to play cards while we waited. I was disappointed to be missing the scene upstairs but, to tell you the truth, I was feeling a bit shaky. I had always found it rather frightening when my mum was drunk, but Great-aunt Dodie, when she was angry, was plain terrifying.

30

Staying with Paulette and Madame Zelda was quite
a relief. The card games were fun, and they gave me
my tea and settled me down for the night. Everyone
thought it was best if I didn't go home, especially
me. I had seen the Perfumed Lady drunk before, but
this time it was different somehow. In the past, she'd
always seemed to be having a good time for most of
it and things turned a bit sour just at the end. You
know, as if she'd been to a really, really good party
and it was only the aftermath of cleaning up the
glasses and the brimming ashtrays that took the edge
off it. Her drinking had always seemed to be like
that, a lot of razzle and a bit of tidying up at the end.

But not this time. This time there was screaming,
crying, puking and bugs and snakes that weren't
really there. Even Auntie Maggie and Uncle Bert

seemed helpless in the face of it. I kept getting flashes of her naked and huddled. She had often seemed helpless but this time she had seemed hopeless too. And her arms – I kept seeing her arms. They were so thin, like sticks they were, and they reminded me of the pictures I had seen of the people Hitler had kept in those terrible camps that nobody thought I ought to know about. Her arms were almost as thin as theirs but nobody had starved her; she must have starved herself. So I was glad I didn't have to go home that night. I wanted to be with people who didn't see snakes and bugs coming out of the walls and who laughed when they played cards.

I don't know when Luigi and Mr Herbert left because I was tucked up in the spare bed by then. Paulette had nipped home for my pyjamas, toothbrush, clean drawers for the morning and my teddy. I know that they stayed for a while after I'd settled down because I heard their laughter coming from the living room. I also heard Sharky join the party. He must have come back to his office rather than go home to wherever it was he lived. I heard Madame Zelda tell him it was a good thing he was around, and that the Perfumed Lady had turned up. She reminded him that Charlie Fluck was expected tomorrow around teatime and suggested that it might be an idea if he made himself available for that particular meeting.

'Worry not, dear lady, I have not forgotten,' I heard him say. 'Neither would I miss it for all the tea in China or, better still, all the brandy in France.' He mumbled something about how all the brandy in France was maybe going too far but that Chinese tea certainly wouldn't keep him away. Then he joined the others in the living room and I nodded off.

It was funny waking up in a strange bed in a strange room. I had just got used to being home from Aggie and now I was away again. It took me a minute to realize that I was merely next door. I lay quietly for a while, trying to hear what was going on, if anything. Judging by the noises from the street, the world was awake and doing, but there was no indication that Paulette and Madame Zelda were. I was thinking about this when my bladder urged me into action. I crept out of my room and was hailed by a cheery Paulette.

'Morning, sweet'eart. What do you fancy for your breakfast? Toast and egg do you? Why don't you join that lazy old bag when you've had your pee and I'll bring it in to you?'

I guessed, correctly as it turned out, that the 'lazy old bag' was Madame Zelda. When I opened the door to her bedroom, she was leaning back against a whole mound of pillows and looking smug.

'Hello, Rosie dear. Jump in. Paulette won't be long. We heard she got the job at Joe Lyon's. Letter came first thing. So she's practisin' her waitressin' on us. Do you reckon she can get it all in 'ere without spillin' a drop? I bet her she couldn't and now she's tryin' to prove me wrong. I ain't as daft as I'm cabbage lookin'. Can't remember the last time I had breakfast in bed.' She gave me a huge wink and patted the bit of bed beside her and heaved a contented sigh. I didn't hang about. I jumped in with her and waited like Lady Muck in miniature.

Paulette won the bet. She didn't spill a drop or misplace a crumb. But when I demanded that Madame Zelda pay up, they both turned bright red. Paulette began to giggle when I went to get Madame Zelda's purse, but when she tried to explain I couldn't really understand because of all their huffing and puffing. Paulette tried to say something about not betting actual money but Madame Zelda hit her with a pillow and I joined in. In the end there were crumbs and tea all over the bed, so we reckoned that nobody had won the bet after all.

*   *   *

Paulette had to go to Joe Lyon's to be fitted for her uniform and to watch the others so that she would be ready to start work on the following day. They told her to be there for half past eleven so that she could watch the busy dinner time. She was really nervous but we helped her choose her clothes and do her hair so that she would arrive looking smart and confident.

We also promised to go to her Corner House for our dinner so that she would see some friendly faces. At least, Madame Zelda promised and I said I'd come too if Auntie Maggie and Uncle Bert would let me. Paulette thought it would be better if Madame Zelda did the checking next door, 'just in case'. I didn't trouble to ask what she meant by that. I knew. It was in case my mum was performing again. I didn't need persuading to stay behind. I made myself useful clearing up the wreckage from our pillow fight and Madame Zelda washed, dressed and went next door.

She was gone about half an hour and returned with clean clothes, permission for me to spend the day with her and the latest news. It seemed that my mum had finally settled down and that they had managed to get her sober enough to understand she had an appointment that she couldn't get out of with

Charlie Fluck at four o'clock. To make sure that she stayed put and sober, everyone except Madame Zelda, Paulette and Mr Herbert was taking it in turns to stay with her. Mr Herbert had his shop to run and Madame Zelda had me to look after.

We went with Paulette to Marble Arch, left her at the corner and promised to be back at one for our dinner. Then we headed to the park, stopping only long enough to buy some bread to feed to the ducks. We had a lovely time, and so did the ducks.

31

We didn't see much of Paulette at Joe Lyon's as she was made to lurk in odd corners so that she didn't get in the way of the Nippies. Joe Lyon's waitresses were always called Nippies, Madame Zelda told me, because they were supposed to nip about very quickly, and they couldn't do that if Paulette was getting under their feet. We didn't see her at all at first, then we noticed her peeping from behind a screen and later she darted behind a potted palm. One poor lady, who was staggering under the weight of a tray piled high with knickerbocker glories, pots of tea and apple pies, was almost decked by Paulette as she flitted to a better lookout.

Madame Zelda and I choked with laughter and sprayed an innocent bystander with sardines on toast. Then we had a fine old time thinking up new names for Nippies now Paulette had joined their ranks. We came up with 'Crashers', 'Crunchers' and 'Bashers' but my favourites were 'Trippies', 'Dodgems' and 'Bruisers'. I really enjoyed that outing; it took my mind off what was going on at home. It also meant that when I thought about Paulette at work, I could picture her in my mind darting between tables and potted palms. It was important to me to be able to 'see' my favourite people when they were away, which was difficult to do if I didn't have a clear picture of where they were.

We dragged out our dinner as long as we could, but this bloke in a really starchy white shirt, black jacket and smart pin-striped trousers kept glaring at us so we left. It was time to head back to the cafe to find out what was going on anyway. For once in my life I wasn't the slightest bit curious. I just wanted it all to go away. Madame Zelda, however, was itching to be around when her ex started shouting the odds. I think she wanted to be the one who slung him out if it came to that. We walked back to the cafe, which took ages because we kept bumping into people we knew. It must have been gone three by the time we arrived.

Things appeared to be normal, but I could tell that Auntie Maggie and Uncle Bert were jumpy. Soon after we arrived, Sharky turned up looking very businesslike; he had brought Muriel with him. She had her notebook in one hand and several pencils, clutched like a bunch of headless flowers, in the other. They sat at the corner table and Uncle Bert joined them. Auntie Maggie and Mrs Wong carried on clearing the decks behind the counter and dishing up the odd cuppa on request. I noticed that Sharky made do with plain coffee for a change; things were obviously very serious.

Madame Zelda and I took a window table so that we could keep an eye out for the first sign of Charlie. The clock's hands crawled round the dial and every time the cafe door opened, heads snapped round to see who it was. At about a quarter to four, the Perfumed Lady and Luigi appeared from upstairs. Someone must have gone to get her some fresh clothes. Instead of the cocktail dress she wore a smart navy-blue suit with a pencil-slim skirt, tailored jacket and a crisp white blouse. Her blond hair was clean and glossy and swept back from her small, pointed face into a French plait. Her nails were freshly painted, not Jezebel this time but a subdued pale pink. She looked a bit like Grace Kelly, sort of cold but good all at the same time.

Her blue eyes seemed huge, with rather fetching

smudges of shadow underneath. They weren't the shocking great black patches she deserved after the night or nights she'd had; they just looked as if she'd had a spot of bother sleeping. I was relieved to see that there wasn't the slightest hint of sick or imaginary snakes and bugs about her. Here, I thought, was a woman who seemed well behaved, efficient and in charge of her life. If I hadn't known better, I'd have sworn that someone had substituted a ringer at the very last minute. Then I noticed that her hands trembled slightly and her eyes had a faraway look as if they were focused on some distant horizon. Closer inspection revealed that they glittered unnaturally, like clean, empty widows. The lights were on but there was no one in.

Later I discovered that Auntie Maggie, Uncle Bert, Luigi and Great-aunt Dodie had had hell's own job to keep her topped up enough to stop the screaming abdabs but not so topped up that she fell over, hurled abuse or dropped her drawers – and not necessarily in that order, according to Auntie Maggie when I heard her telling Paulette about it.

Just before four o'clock Uncle Bert cleared out the last of the punters and changed the door sign to 'closed'. Great-aunt Dodie arrived with Mr Herbert, who must have shut up his shop early. Mamma and

Papa Campanini appeared with several sons and sons-in-law, and Maltese Joe sent a bevy of his less obvious henchmen, including Frankie. It seemed that everyone wanted in on the act. I realized that the stealing of my adoption papers and the inclusion of Dave in Charlie's scheme, whatever that was, had added something to the situation that made us and ours close ranks.

We all knew that Dave was an evil bugger, and there was no love lost between us and him. Uncle Bert was expecting trouble and this was a show of strength. However, it was decided not to be blatant about it and the crowd was quickly supplied with drinks and tables in the faint hope that they could pass for ordinary punters. I changed the 'closed' sign back to 'open' to complete the stage setting.

The bugger was late.

It was well gone five o'clock and the cafe was still stiff with suspiciously muscular punters, but there was no Charlie Fluck. The troops sat around in groups depending on whose boys they were: the Campanini lot were camped around Luigi, Mamma and Papa; Maltese Joe's sat at two tables, bickering about some bet or other; Auntie Maggie had given up all pretence of working and sat with Sharky; Muriel, the Perfumed Lady and Uncle Bert were at the corner table; and Madame Zelda and I had our window seats. We had been joined by Great-aunt Dodie and Mr Herbert. I noticed that the Perfumed Lady was staying well clear of her formidable aunt.

Mrs Wong carried on with her chores as if nothing was happening, but I noticed that she was in no rush to leave. Mrs Wong was like that; you never really knew what she was thinking. She carried on through everything as if she hadn't seen what was going on. She didn't smile much, or scowl for that matter. In fact she rarely spoke, but I'm pretty sure she understood English as well as anybody; she just didn't let on. Mrs Wong and I both knew that people talked much more freely if they thought you didn't understand them.

The only way to find out anything abut Mrs Wong was to watch her carefully. Her actions told you what she was thinking. I always knew she was fond of me, for instance. Whenever I was poorly, she'd bring me little Chinese treats like paper flowers that opened as if by magic when you put them in water, or sparklers or a tin of lychees. But she was never a hugger or a kisser like Auntie Maggie, Madame Zelda or Paulette. It just wasn't her way.

If she didn't like you, there was no telling what she'd do. I saw her spit in Dave's tea once when he'd called her a 'Chinky slag' and told her to hurry up. I never told a soul. It was our little secret, and he deserved it. She rarely looked directly at anyone either. In fact it was the way she *didn't* look at you that told you what she thought of you. If you were one of those people she really didn't like, like Dave, then she looked right through you as if you weren't there, and she didn't seem to hear you either. If she was indifferent to you, it was as if she was looking at someone over your shoulder. She would hear you, though, and give you your order soon as you asked. If she liked you, then she'd sort of look at you but not straight into your face and her lips might twitch very slightly. You've heard of a half-smile? Well, Mrs Wong's twitch was a hundredth of a smile, and you had to be quick to catch it. Once, when I was crying fit to bust and Auntie Maggie and Uncle Bert were temporarily missing, she stroked my hair and made funny little clicking noises. It is the only time I ever remember her touching me unless it was to wipe my mush or put a plaster on my knee.

When Charlie finally did turn up, it was a bit of a let-down. It was just on six o'clock. He came alone so the troops were unnecessary, as it turned out. He sort of sidled in the door as if he knew the punters were no ordinary punters, and he looked nervous.

His odd eyes darted from group to group, his Adam's apple kept bobbing up and down as he swallowed anxiously, and he made straight for the corner table and Uncle Bert. He noticed me sitting with Madame Zelda and Great-aunt Dodie, but he tried hard to ignore us all. I think seeing Great-aunt Dodie gave him a bit of a start, and confirmed his suspicion that I was Cassandra's mysterious child.

Uncle Bert eyed Charlie with obvious dislike and reluctantly introduced him to my mum and Sharky. Without discussion, Madame Zelda and Great-aunt Dodie – those two formidable women – went to stand each side of Charlie, who shrank visibly. He hadn't reckoned on a reception committee and was not a happy man. I got up from my seat too, walked around the table and planted myself on Mr Herbert's lap. I watched from there, thumb in mouth. I really didn't want to get too close.

There was a bit of shuffling around to make room for Charlie to sit down. Great-aunt Dodie and Madame Zelda remained standing. There was a murmur of conversation that went on for some time and then, to the astonishment of the rest of us, my mum began to laugh. She literally rocked backwards and forwards and tears streamed down her face.

Charlie went red and blustered. No one else at the corner table even smiled.

Once she'd subsided, Charlie said something else and my mum burst out so we could all hear loud and clear, 'Don't be such an idiot. Do you *really* think I give a damn what that lot think? Let you have my shares? Are you mad? And if you manage to get your greedy hands on them, what then? Planning to sell them to Godfrey, are you? Over my dead body! Why don't you just bugger off back to the hole you climbed out of, there's a good little man. If you want to blackmail someone you really ought to find out if they care about their secret for a start. You should've done your homework, sweetheart, then you'd know I am utterly indifferent to my mother's opinion, or that of her friends for that matter. You can tell the world for all I care!'

She threw back her head and began to laugh again. There was something very scary about that laugh; it had a touch of the nutter about it. Charlie, however, was not amused. He leaped to his feet, knocking his chair over as he did so, and made for the door, red-faced and blowing like an asthmatic weasel. He almost knocked Madame Zelda over in his charge for the way out.

He wrenched the door open, then delivered his

parting shot. 'You can laugh now, but you'll be laughin' on the other side of your kisser when I'm finished with you. Let's see how you feel when I tell your mum and stepdad that you've gorn and given their only grandchild away. Let's face it, that raving iron of a brother of yours ain't going to be breedin', now is he?' He took a familiar-looking sheet of paper from his pocket and waved it in the air. 'You reckon this bit of bog paper will stand up in court once your lot start chucking their money at it, do you? Well, we'll just see about that!'

Just then, a knife whistled through the air and pinned the paper to the door frame. Charlie was left, white as a sheet, with only a torn corner of the paper in his upraised hand. Everyone looked at one another, bewildered. Who had thrown that knife? It had happened so fast that no one had seen it coming. We'd all been too busy looking at Charlie.

'I s'pose you think you're clever. Well, you can't frighten me,' said Charlie, looking thoroughly frightened. 'I'll be back with another copy of that paper so you wasted your bleedin' energy chuckin' shivs about.'

He slammed the cafe door as he left. There was silence for a few moments and then all hell broke loose. Everyone was talking at once. Frankie asked

Uncle Bert if he wanted Charlie brought back, beaten up or what? And the Campaninis were checking with one another to see if any of them had thrown the knife.

The Perfumed Lady was still laughing her head off in that weird way when the door opened again. Paulette was back from her shift at Joe Lyon's. She stood in the doorway looking in bewilderment from us to the knife and the paper flapping gently in the breeze. Eventually she gave herself a little shake, as if coming out of a trance, and yanked the blade out of the door frame. With the knife in one hand and the paper in the other, she asked with a smile if they belonged to anyone.

Uncle Bert pulled himself together and collected the knife and the now-tatty adoption agreement from Paulette. 'Ta for being here, all of you. I'm sure your ugly kissers helped the toe-rag to see that he was outclassed as well as outnumbered. Now if you would be so kind, I reckon it's time to close up for the day. We've got some serious thinking to do.'

With that, the mob of borrowed heavies trailed out, promising to be on call for any future run-ins with Charlie Fluck and pals, assuming he had any.

Only our nearest and dearest were left clustered around our corner table and nobody had much to say for a bit, especially me. I was frozen, numbed by a combination of fear and guilt. It was really difficult to grasp how I had managed to cause so much trouble for everyone. It seemed to me at that moment, and for the first time in my short life, that it would have been better if I'd never been born.

32

Once Uncle Bert had the knife in his horny mitt, it became obvious who must have thrown it. It was one of our kitchen knives, used for slicing stuff thinly, and had been sharpened so often that it was worn almost to a stiletto. The point was, only Mrs Wong was still behind the counter and in a position to lay a hand on the thing. Uncle Bert and Auntie Maggie had both been sitting at the corner table when it had whistled through the air, almost parting Charlie's barnet for him.

Uncle Bert looked in awe at the knife in his hand and then at the space where Mrs Wong had been. She'd managed to glide out when everyone else had left and we hadn't noticed.

Uncle Bert whistled through his teeth. 'Well, I'll be buggered,' he muttered to no one in particular.

'Remind me not to get on the wrong side of Mrs Wong, will you?'

After the troops had left, only the usual mob remained, with the addition of Sharky and Muriel. They were cordially invited to stay for the evening as there was much to discuss. The Perfumed Lady was showing signs of restlessness, however. She began to talk about leaving but she was told in no uncertain terms that she wasn't going anywhere until things had been sorted, once and for all.

'Listen, love,' Auntie Maggie explained gently. 'I know the last day or two have been hard on you, but we need you where we can lay hands on you in a hurry. If we let you out of here, there's no telling when we'll track you down again and what state you'll be in when we do find you. You know what a flighty piece you can be. The little bugger will be back and there's no saying what his next scheme will be like. At least stay and talk things over so we can make some sort of plan.'

Great-aunt Dodie was not so kind. 'Yes, Cassandra, we need you here for the time being. I also think it is long past time for some explanations, don't you?' My mum opened her mouth to protest but Great-aunt Dodie held up her hand for silence. 'Please don't start *whining*, Cassandra, and listen. If

Clunt insists on involving Godfrey, and there's every indication that he has already, there's no predicting what he will do. The thing is, you've shirked your responsibilities long enough. It is time to grow up and face them.'

My mum started pacing like a caged animal. 'I'm not staying here for bloody ever. I have a life too, you know. It might not seem much to you but *I* like it and I want to get on with it. I went to great lengths to get away from Godfrey and my mother and I have no intention of ever seeing either of them again. So get that into your heads right now.'

But Great-aunt Dodie had what I shall always think of as that 'Afghan' look in her eyes. 'Oh do shut up,' she said, 'there's a good girl. What makes you think we're even mildly interested in what passes for your life? There will still be men and gin out there when we've finished with you. And Clunt's right; heirs from Charles are most unlikely. Not only do you have to secure Rosa's future but you must think of your shares in the family business as well. It would suit Godfrey to have another ally, however young. Has it ever occurred to you how very useful Rosa would be to him if he could get his hands on her?'

This little speech had the most astounding effect

on the Perfumed Lady. She had absolute hysterics. She began to thrash about blindly, screaming at us all that nothing on earth was going to make her have anything to do with Godfrey or the business, so we had better get used to the idea. Then she grabbed her handbag and made a break for the door. If Great-aunt Dodie hadn't been so nippy on her feet, she'd have made it too. It took Auntie Maggie, Madame Zelda and Great-aunt Dodie to get her back, still shrieking like a banshee. She really didn't like Godfrey, you could tell. What's more, she was obviously deeply afraid of him.

I was still sitting on Mr Herbert's lap when she started ranting and throwing herself about, and for a moment she looked as though she was going to grab hold of me. Very gently he stood me on the floor, then led me by the hand upstairs out of the way. It was kind of him as he must have realized that she scared me. We could still hear her, though. It took ages and several stiff gins to calm her down.

I'm not sure what else happened that night. Auntie Maggie came upstairs after a while and put me to bed. She must have forgotten that I'd had no tea and she looked so worried that I didn't like to remind her. Luckily, Mr Herbert and I had raided the biscuit tin on the way upstairs, so I wasn't starving to actual *death*.

What with one thing and another, we'd all forgotten that I was supposed to be at school the Monday Charlie had turned up. This meant that I was a day late and missed choosing a seat by the window with my mates. I ended up having to share a desk with Enie Smales. Yuk! Enie always smelled of stale pee and unwashed clothes. I was far from thrilled and laid the blame squarely on Charlie Fluck and the Perfumed Lady.

Auntie Maggie was unusually flustered on the Tuesday morning as she got me ready. She had to go into school to explain why I had been missing. We didn't tell them the truth, of course, our business being none of theirs, but made something up about a visit from my long-lost great-aunt, which had the virtue of being sort of true. She *had* visited us on that Monday and she *had* been long-lost. We didn't trouble to mention that we'd seen tons of her over the last few weeks. Funny the distinctions that grown-ups make about lying. If a kid does it, then it's automatically bad, bad, bad. If a grown-up they don't like does it and gets found out, the same rules apply, only more so. If they do it themselves, however, it is perfectly understandable and is one of those famous 'white lies' you hear so much about. Anyway, we bent the truth to fit our needs and you could say we were punished; but more about that later.

To an outsider, it might have seemed that things got back to normal pretty quickly after Charlie's visit, but they didn't. First off, everyone was jumpy; we knew we hadn't heard the last of Charlie and his schemes. Also, we knew exactly where my mum was.

Now, knowing the whereabouts of the Perfumed Lady when she wasn't lolling in our spare bed or throwing up in our khazi was not easy. We *never* knew where she was unless she was under our feet, so to speak. This time we did. Great-aunt Dodie had marched her off to a clinic near Harley Street where she was locked up. She was kept away from booze, drugs and men and fed at regular intervals, so my great-aunt said. I was very worried that locking her up was a bit like putting her in prison and that it was cruel. Auntie Maggie said it wasn't as simple as that. She was ill and needed caring for for a while.

I knew this was true but to *lock her up*? I wasn't at all sure about that bit. I must admit that my concern was pretty selfish. If she got locked up for being ill, what would happen to me next time I was poorly? It was a big worry. However, both Auntie Maggie and Uncle Bert assured me that security was not that good and if she *really, really* wanted to leg it, she could. They reckoned that although she was complaining long and loud, part of her wanted to be kept in a safe place. They thought that the attack of the screaming abdabs had made her stop and think a bit. They explained that what ailed my mum was not the same thing at all as measles, mumps or chicken-pox and that I needn't worry about being locked away myself. It was a relief. It was also untrue as it turned out, but they weren't to know that.

The first week or so of the new term was a bit of a blur. Not only was I stuck next to Smelly Smales (I'm ashamed to say her nickname was my idea), but things were tense at home too. I do remember our new teacher, Miss Hampton, though. She was weird; pale, fey and from the Fen country. We did a lot of geography, history and English about the Fens before she disappeared without trace after half-term. To this day, Miss Hampton's face is imprinted on my brain. You see, her disappearance was connected to me in a way.

We were playing in the playground about three weeks after term started. In fact, it was *exactly* three weeks after it started; even I couldn't be vague about that. We had all been playing and Miss Hampton was on playground duty. The rest of the school had just filed in because the end-of-play bell had rung. Our class was last, being as how our teacher was on duty.

Anyway, there we were, just our class and Miss Hampton, when two blokes in masks appeared from around the side of the building. One was armed with a socking great knife and grabbed Miss Hampton and held it to her throat. He growled at us not to scream or make a sound otherwise he'd let her have it. Now Miss Hampton hadn't exactly endeared herself to us, she was too strange for that, but we didn't want her throat cut in front of us either. So we kept our gobs shut, more or less, although one or two of us snivelled a bit. Naturally Smelly Smales had snot down to her knees in seconds, she was that kind of kid. The other bloke looked us all over, then he grabbed me and stuck his hand over my mouth and started dragging me towards the school gate.

I was too shocked to say or do anything. I recognized my bloke straight away. He had odd eyes, one blue, one brown. It was Charlie Fluck. Thinking back, I was paralysed with terror, which was why I didn't struggle. The knife man followed, dragging Miss Hampton with him. I was thrown into the back of a black car and Charlie jumped in next to me. The other man reached the gate and sort of slung Miss Hampton away, so she stumbled and fell just inside the playground. He jumped into the seat beside the driver.

'Move it, you stupid cow!' he yelled, as he slammed the car door. I could tell by her smell that the driver was a woman; she used Evening in Paris. And, of course, nobody calls a bloke a 'stupid cow'. I recognized the knife man's voice. It was Dave, and I was very afraid.

Charlie pushed me down into the seat so that no one could see me and we shot away like bats out of hell. I think we were in Shaftesbury Avenue after zigzagging a bit. I know we went up the Charing Cross Road because I could just see one or two rooftops and I recognized the front of the cinema on the corner of Sutton Row. We turned left into Oxford Street. Once we were past Marble Arch, though, I lost track.

We twisted and turned but it wasn't too long before the car stopped and I was bundled up some stairs and into a flat. I was shivering and shaking by this time and, like Smelly Smales, I'd wet myself. The two men didn't remove their masks but the one I thought was Dave smacked me in the mouth and told me to shut up. I tried, honest I did, but huge sobs kept escaping. He clouted me again but I still couldn't stop. In the end, he threw me into a tiny room with no windows and locked the door.

It was a large cupboard, I think, because there were shelves. I don't know how long I was in there. It felt like ages.

33

There was nothing to see or do in that cupboard and if I let my mind wander I started to feel sick with fear. So I began reciting my tables to keep my imagination quiet. It was pretty boring and I must have dozed off because the next thing I knew, Dave was shouting on the other side of the door.

'I could've *told* you that her mother was a whore, you prick. There was me thinking you knew what the hell you were doing. But oh no, you had to go and advertise. Now she's been snatched, that Bert Featherby will be on to us in a flash. You had better get in touch with that geezer right now. We've got to offload the brat and quick. If Bert's lot catch us at it, I wouldn't give a rat's arse for our chances.'

'Put him down, Dave,' said a woman's voice.

'Look at him, he's all red in the kisser. If you choke the life out of him, we're stuck with the kid. We don't know who the hell Charlie's boss is, remember, let alone where he is and how to get hold of the bugger. Let him go, can't you?'

There was a thud. Then I heard Charlie's voice whining, 'All right, all right. There's no need to get yer hair off. He's expecting me to call him anyway. He knows about her and he's expecting to see her while he's here. OK, he wasn't home when I got on the blower but his missis thinks he'll be back this afternoon some time. Give it another hour or so and I'll give him another go.'

'Listen to me, you double-dyed prat and a half,' Dave shouted. 'The longer we have the kid the bigger shtook we're in. I'm telling you, Bert Featherby is connected and I mean *connected*. Him and Maltese Joe have been tight since they were kids together. They used to run with the same mob and that Featherby has got Joe out of more than one spot of bother in his time. He also stopped him from being knocked off at least once that I heard about.

'They're almost like brothers and I'm telling you Maltese Joe owes him big. He will move everything and everyone he's got to find her. He owns half the bleeding filth at West End Central nick for starters, not to mention his boys, and then there's the favours all the other bleeding wops owe him. No, mate, you're not leaving it no hour. You go round there and you camp on his doorstep if necessary till he shows.'

'OK, OK, if you're that bleedin' scared. But I might as well take the brat with me and then he and his missis can just cough up and take her with them.'

'Do you think I was born yesterday?' Dave shouted again. 'You ain't taking the kid anywhere. Go there and ring us when it's settled. Arrange a meet. Theresa will bring the brat and when you pass over our cut, you get the kid and not before. What you and this boss of yours do with her after that is your business. Me and Theresa are away, mate. You don't have the first idea of who you are up against, no idea at all. Maltese Joe eats people like you and me for breakfast. We could end up as part of the fucking foundations of a new corporation piss 'ole, and I ain't kidding. The man does not mess about.'

Shortly after that, I heard the front door slam. I thought about what I had heard. It was a relief to know that Uncle Bert and Maltese Joe were bound to be looking for me. Auntie Maggie would have been expecting me back for my dinner, so they would have missed me by now. My belly was busy telling me with rumbles and gurgles that it was way past dinner time.

I sucked my thumb for a bit, partly for comfort and partly for something to stick in my gob. It also stopped me from sobbing out loud. Thoughts of Auntie Maggie had brought on the tears again and I didn't want to attract Dave's attention. I was deeply afraid of him. It had something to do with his cold, dead eyes and the beatings that poor Paulette had taken in the past. My sobs were just beginning to get to the heaving stage when I heard the sound of a telephone ringing very close at hand. Theresa answered it.

'I *know* it's you, Charlie. Who else could it be? Say that again. Hang about, I'll ask him. Dave, Charlie says bring her to the Corner House at Marble Arch at three. He says his boss wants to talk to her to make sure she really is that posh slag's kid, then he'll cough up the dough. What do you say? Hang on, Charlie, he's coming to the blower now. All right, all right, there's no need to break me fingers, is there?'

'I'll break your bleeding jaw if you don't shut it,' I

308

heard Dave say. 'What? Speak up for Christ's sake, I can't hear you. OK, three it is. And Charlie, no funny business. Theresa'll bring the kid and hang about while they rabbit. I'll be outside, keeping my eye on the door. Give her the money when he's satisfied and that'll be it. If anything goes wrong, bring the kid out with you and we'll go from there. Oh, and Charlie, if it all goes to plan, I'd piss off smartish if I was you and keep your head down. Right, three it is.'

Time seemed to crawl past after that and my belly rumbled louder and louder. At last the door was opened and there was Theresa, all smiles. 'Come on, lovey. Time to go. Oh my Gawd, you've peed yourself. Dave, she's wet herself and she's in a right old state. We'll have to get her something to wear.'

'What do you mean, "get her something to wear"? If you think I'm spending anything on her, you're out of your crust. Let's just get shot of her and call it a day.'

'But, Dave, if they're as posh as Charlie says, won't it look a bit funny if she's all wet behind? Specially at the Corner House. They might not even let us in if she's in that state. She only needs a pair of knickers and a skirt or something.'

'All right, but make it snappy. Sling her back in the cupboard and nip down the road to that place on the corner. Here you are, that'll have to cover it. I'm not chucking dosh away. We'll need every bloody penny if this goes wrong.'

I was pushed back into my prison and the door was slammed.

A little while later, Theresa was back with this horrible pair of knickers and this skirt made of orange gingham. It looked really disgusting with my pale blue school shirt. I preferred my gymslip and that's saying something. I insisted on folding my soggy knickers and damp gymslip carefully and putting them in the bag my new clothes came in. Theresa took me to the bathroom for another pee and a bit of a wash. I stank a bit anyway, and still had blood on my mush from when Dave hit me.

She finished me off by combing my hair. You can't comb curly hair with just an ordinary comb, as it yanks it out by the roots. It shows how scared I was that I didn't even yell. I didn't want Dave to hit me again. He could pack a wallop, I'll say that for him. At least, I thought he could, but then nobody had ever hit me before, except other kids at school and they didn't count.

At last we were ready to go. My heart was hammering. The Corner House at Marble Arch. I was pretty sure they meant Joe Lyon's and maybe Paulette would be there. I started praying like the clappers that she would be.

34

We walked to Marble Arch. It turned out that we were just around the corner from it. Dave was nervous, I could tell; his eyes were everywhere at once and he was sweating. He was afraid we'd be seen by someone who knew Uncle Bert or, worse, Maltese Joe. We were very close to our own manor after all. They had me between them. Dave had hold of my wrist so hard I thought he was going to break it, and Theresa held my hand. I suppose, looking back, they were trying to look like a happy little family on a day out. Naturally Dave had taken his mask off by then as people would have noticed and thought it was funny. It took less than ten minutes to get to the meeting place. I was right, the Corner House was Paulette's Joe Lyon's. My heart leaped with hope.

Once we were outside, Dave took an even firmer grip on me. 'Now you behave, you little snot, or I won't think twice about slinging you under a bus,' he snarled. 'Theresa, get in there and look around to make sure they're there. Walk up to 'em if they are and ask if they have the money. If the answer's yes, come and get the kid. If it's no, tell them they have one hour to get it and no funny business if they want to see her alive. Got that?'

Theresa nodded, let go of my hand and disappeared inside.

I was really worried that she would see Paulette. She hated Paulette and it would ruin my chances if she saw her. I wasn't so worried about Charlie. He had hardly ever seen her and anyway they had never spoken to each other.

I prayed while we waited. 'Please, God, don't let Charlie have recognized our Paulette, if she's there,' I said over and over again. I reckon God must've heard, because Paulette said later that Charlie looked straight at her and there wasn't a flicker.

Theresa of course was another kettle of fish. I started praying all over again. I promised God anything, I can tell you. I swore that if he kept Paulette out of sight while Theresa was in there then I'd help Auntie Maggie more and never ever be naughty again, and lobbed in promises never to swear, pick my nose or listen at doorways while I was at it. (I'm ashamed to say that, as time went on, I forgot all my promises and slipped back into my bad old ways, but luckily God didn't seem to mind a lot.)

As Theresa went into Joe Lyon's, my heart was in my mouth. It seemed *years* before she came out again but of course it was only minutes. She told Dave that they were there and that they had showed her a great wad of notes in an envelope.

Just then, Charlie came out too. 'The boss says make it snappy, Dave. He has things to do. He just wants to talk to the kid, then if he's satisfied, Theresa'll bring your dosh out. I've got to go and get his Roller. Wish I could say it's been nice knowing yer, but I don't reckon it has, so I won't. TTFN, Theresa, I hope we bump into each other again one day.' And he was gone.

Dave muttered something about a prick and gave Theresa a shove. 'Go on then, you stupid cow. Let's get this over.' He looked down at me with those awful, cold eyes of his. 'And you, just tell the man who your mum is and don't mess about if you know what's good for you. Theresa'll bring you straight out again if you give her any trouble, then you'll have *me* to deal with. I ain't intending to take you with us, so if we're stuck with you, it's under a bus and sharpish. Now piss off, the pair of you.'

Once we got inside the door, Theresa knelt down beside me, gave my hair a little tweak and whispered, 'He means it, love, so be a good girl and do as he says. He hates your auntie Maggie and uncle Bert, so he's itching to have a go at you. Don't give him the satisfaction, love. Just tell the man who your mum is and you'll be fine. I promise, the first chance I get, I'll ring Sharky Finn and tell him who's got you. Come on now.' She took me by the hand and led me through the tables to the back of the restaurant.

I kept looking around, hoping to see Paulette and signal to her, but she was nowhere to be seen. I began to worry that she wasn't at work that day and my heart sank. I was so miserable that it took me a minute to realize that we had stopped at a table at the back, tucked away in the corner. The man sitting at the table had slicked-back dark hair and yellow skin. He had a sharp nose and funny, almost yellow eyes. The colour was just like our Tom's, and they looked at me the way Tom looked at a mouse when he was batting it back and forth between his paws.

I shuddered and my heart hit my socks. I looked at the woman next. It was funny, that. Mostly you expect to notice the woman first. I think it's because they wear more interesting clothes and bright colours and make-up. But this woman was so colourless, she almost wasn't there. Her skin was the colour of putty; her hair was pale brown, mousy they call it, and wispy. She was very, very thin. Then I noticed her eyes. They were exactly like the Perfumed Lady's, only tired and lifeless. They reminded me of the eyes of those fish you see at the fishmonger's, but blue.

The man spoke first. 'Who damaged her? How did she get that split lip and the bruises?' It seemed a strange word to use. Most people would have said 'hurt' or 'who hit her', not 'damaged'. He made me sound like a bit of china or a piece of furniture. He didn't sound like he was talking about a real live person at all. It made my skin crawl.

The pale woman smiled a faded sort of smile. 'She looks just like Cassandra at that age, doesn't she, Godfrey?' She'd have said more but the man gave her such a withering look she shut up immediately.

'I said, who damaged her?'

'My boyfriend did. He's not very patient with kids and she was crying. He wanted to shut her up.'

The man thought about this, then reached out and took my chin in his hand and turned my face first one way and then the other. His face was expressionless, like a yellow, waxy mask, and his hand was very cold. He picked up a thick white envelope that was lying on the table among the remains of their tea. He opened it slowly and removed several big, white, crinkly notes and placed them carefully in the wallet that he took from the inside pocket of his jacket.

'Tell this boyfriend of yours that I pay less for damaged goods. It has cost him a hundred.'

Theresa began to say that she'd been told to take me straight out again if there was any funny business.

He raised his hand slightly. 'Be quiet, woman. I'm sure your man friend will realize that nine hundred is better than nothing at all, and what would he do with the child if you took her back? Kill her? Messy, don't you think? No profit and a murder charge. Surely neither of you is that stupid? Take the money and go. We are satisfied that she is who you say she is.' He turned away from her, dismissing her as if she was a servant.

Theresa hesitated for just a second, then bent down slightly to talk to me. 'Be good, Rosie. These nice people will take care of you. Remember what I said before.' She turned and left. We all watched her go without a word.

The man told me to sit down. It was then that I caught a glimpse of Paulette. I saw her reflection in one of the mirrors that lined the walls. She was hiding behind a pillar until Theresa was safely out of the way, and she was talking to another Nippy, who looked across at us and nodded.

I kept looking in the mirror as if I was staring blankly at nothing, although I was watching her every move. The man and woman talked quietly to each other. My heart was hammering and I felt faint with relief. She knew I was there and she knew it was wrong. She would save me, I knew it!

The part of me that wasn't watching Paulette was listening to the conversation the couple were having.

'But, Godfrey, how will we explain the fact they just took her? Isn't kidnap illegal?'

Godfrey heaved a sigh, then explained in the patient tone that people use when they're being sarky, 'Yes, Evelyn, kidnap is illegal, but we shall simply explain that we paid the ransom to get her back. We had nothing at all to do with the crime and we can prove that. We shall return her to her home of course. We will merely give them time to reach the desired pitch of anxiety. People will agree to all sorts of things if they are anxious enough.'

'But, Godfrey, how will we explain her bruises?

They might not be so willing to agree to anything at all if they see she's been hurt. Can't we take her home with us, just until she heals?'

'Don't be any more of a fool than you can help. Of course we can't just take her with us right now. But Carstairs is a good man and he assures me that custody will be relatively easy to get. Her mother is a drunken prostitute and these foster parents are unrelated and lower class. The court is bound to view our request favourably. We can offer her considerable advantages: wealth, privilege and a good private education. Her foster parents may even see sense all by themselves and we may not have to resort to the law. Who knows? We shall find out soon enough.'

Just then, Paulette came over to the table. 'Hello, Rosie, I thought it was you. What are you doing here? Do Maggie and Bert know where you are, dear?'

I had opened my mouth to reply when the nasty yellow man shoved his oar in. 'Waitress, I do not believe that we asked for your assistance, but now that you are here perhaps you will bring our bill.'

'Certainly, sir. I'll just hear what Rosie has to say, if you don't mind. We know each other very well, you see. We're neighbours and I don't believe I have ever had the pleasure of meeting either of you. You will understand, sir, that I am concerned when I see my young friend battered and bruised and in the company of strangers.'

I was ever so impressed. Paulette didn't get flustered and she sounded so posh and in command of herself.

Godfrey's eyes flickered like a snake's, or at least how I imagined a snake's eyes would flicker. (I'm afraid of snakes. Luckily, I had only seen one once and that was round someone's neck. Paulette said it was a python.) Then Godfrey smiled for the very first time – if you could call it a smile. His mouth stretched sideways but his smile never reached those awful eyes.

'Your concern is very commendable. My wife is the child's grandmother and I am her step-grandfather, if there is such a relationship. Now, if you are satisfied, we will have our bill please.' Another tight smile.

'Certainly, sir, but Rosie still hasn't had the opportunity to answer me. Rosie, are these your grandparents, step or otherwise, and are you happy to be with them?'

Once again, I had my gob open to answer when

Godfrey barged in. His voice was sharp and had the tone of one who was used to issuing orders and having others leap to do as they were told.

'That is enough, young lady. I have given you all the answers you are going to get. Now, the bill, please, or must I call the manager?'

Paulette was magnificent. 'That won't be necessary, sir. I see the police have arrived at last. Perhaps you would care to explain it all to them.' She turned to me. 'Don't worry, Rosie my love, your auntie Maggie and uncle Bert know you're safe. The manager telephoned Sharky. They should be here in a second or two.' She turned back to Ghastly Godfrey. 'I'm sure that you do not wish to cause a scene, sir, so if you will just accompany me to the manager's office you can explain everything to the officers. As you may have noticed, some more officers are waiting at the door, should you decide to try to leave in a hurry.'

I was so relieved by this time that I even managed to look at the people at the tables around us. They were gobsmacked, peepers wide like astonished owls and their mouths forming silent Os. I swear several jaws hit the floor.

Evelyn's pasty face was white as she looked towards Godfrey's yellow one for reassurance. She didn't get any. His expression was grim but calm. He rose from the table without looking at any of us and waited for Evelyn and me to join him. Once we were assembled to his satisfaction, he barged Paulette aside. 'Get out of the way, woman,' he hissed. 'I take it the office is over there?' He pointed towards a brown door almost hidden behind a palm at the back of the enormous room.

Paulette smiled politely. 'If you will follow me, sir, I'll show you.'

We moved off towards the front of the restaurant and some stairs that I hadn't noticed before that were almost hidden behind a serving station where the clean cutlery, china and glasses were kept. We looked like a small crocodile of kids trailing off to the headmistress's study for a really serious telling-off. Only Ghastly Godfrey looked confident but I knew that was about to change. My auntie Maggie and uncle Bert would want to kill him, or worse, when they got their mitts on him, I was absolutely sure of that.

The stairs to the manager's office were dark and steep and I kept stumbling in my hurry to get there. I was dying to see Auntie Maggie and Uncle Bert.

Paulette was still in the lead and I hugged her side. There wasn't a snowflake's chance in hell that I was going to let her out of my sight until I had my aunt, uncle or preferably both of them within reach.

At last we got to this brown door and Paulette knocked politely and waited. A voice said, 'Come in,' and we went in.

The room was stiff with people and I looked anxiously from face to face to find the ones I loved. The best I could come up with was one I liked a lot. T.C.'s reassuring figure stepped out of the scrum and I hurled myself at his knees, sobbing frantically. He lifted me up and held me close for what seemed like ages and I could have sworn I felt something warm and wet where my cheek met his.

Eventually I needed air and squirmed a bit and looked around me. There was a policewoman, four burly great coppers, a cowering Charlie, Paulette, Ghastly Godfrey, Evelyn and Mr Frobisher, Paulette's boss, besides T.C. and me. Then we heard footsteps on the stairs and a familiar puffing and panting and there, in the doorway, was my beloved auntie Maggie, closely followed by Uncle Bert.

Looks of pure joy flashed across their faces as they saw me in T.C.'s arms. Then they seemed taken aback, surprised even. I suppose it was my bruising and the split lip. I slid down T.C. and crossed the room and winded poor Auntie Maggie as I hit her at speed. I clung like a limpet, howling with relief. It took a while and a gobstopper from my left lug to calm me down and to dry me off from tears and kisses.

Eventually, T.C. got down to business. He flashed his warrant card at Ghastly Godfrey and that vapid half-wit Evelyn. 'I must ask you to accompany me to the station to make your statements concerning the abduction of the child known as Rosa Featherby from her school earlier today. There is also the question of a serious armed assault on a Miss Hampton during that abduction. I should warn you that although you are not under arrest at this stage, what you say may still be used in evidence.'

With that, he nodded at the four burly coppers and they marched Charlie, Godfrey and Evelyn away. No one went quietly. Charlie wheedled, blaming everyone and their brothers. Evelyn wrung her hands and leaked information along with her tears. 'I *told* you kidnap was a crime, Godfrey,' she whined. And all the while Godfrey hissed at her to be quiet, just like the snake he so reminded me of.

Only T.C. and the policewoman stayed behind when they left. He looked solemn. 'I'm sorry, Bert, Maggie. Little Rosie will have to come to the station as well to make a statement. Naturally you can come with her. We'll try not to keep her long. You must want to get her home. You'll have to come as well, Paulette, to tell us what you saw and heard. And, by the way, well done for calling us immediately. You're the heroine of the hour.'

Paulette went bright red and I began to moan. 'I don't wanna go anywhere, I want my dinner, I'm starving!' I said in a rush.

For some reason everyone laughed, and that nice Mr Frobisher gave me egg, bacon, a fried slice and chips on the house, followed by a socking great knickerbocker glory.

With a huge but contented belly, I felt much more like making my statement to T.C. and the police-woman, Mary. She let me wear her hat all the way to the station.

Oh, the relief of seeing the cafe again! I went straight up to my room, tore off the hated knickers and the awful orange skirt and demanded a bath. It must have been a first, that; me demanding a bath.

I slept in Auntie Maggie's and Uncle Bert's bed that night and for many, many nights after.

I didn't go to school for a while either, I was too afraid to let my auntie Maggie and uncle Bert out of my sight and, if the truth was known, I don't think they wanted me out of theirs either.

35

Of course, we hadn't heard the last of it.

Great-aunt Dodie appeared the next day saying that Godfrey and Evelyn hadn't even been kept in prison for the night. There hadn't been enough evidence to hold them. Nobody could relax with those two on the loose and, sure enough, within a week we received a letter from a solicitor called Carstairs, saying that my mum was 'a drunkard and a moral degenerate' and that they, as my grandparents, would be seeking custody.

There was an emergency meeting in the cafe, but Sharky was confident. 'Ah, but what they don't know yet, but will within the hour, is that Charlie boy sang like the chorus at Covent Garden. Word perfect he was too. They've caught Dave and Theresa. It seems that the lovely Theresa is somewhat disenchanted with our David and is giving the magnificient T.C. chapter, verse and page numbers even as I sit here gasping for my coffee.'

I wasn't allowed to go to court when the case came up months later, but I heard plenty about it afterwards. I was sort of playing by the cafe window but really keeping a lookout for my tribe, so I was there when they burst in, gabbling with triumph.

'Fancy him thinking he was Rosie's father.' My heart froze in my chest as Madame Zelda said those words. But she quickly thawed it again. 'The numbers ain't right, as he would know if only he'd asked when her birthday was. The look that wife of his shot him, he should have withered up right there. I reckon there'll be trouble in paradise on visiting days, I do. That's if she troubles herself with visiting days. If I was married to that reptile, it'd be "good riddance to bad rubbish" and I'd be away on me toes.'

'No wonder our Cassie took off like that,' Auntie Maggie cut in. 'When T.C. got her to tell him what had happened back home he told her she could have charged that stepfather with rape. T.C. met her soon after she hit the Smoke. He found her soliciting near that bomb-site where Cliff's bookshop used to be; felt sorry for her, he said. But she didn't want to know about pressing any charges, just wanted to stay away from him, no matter what. Terrible really, when you think about the turn her life took and what she could've been.' Auntie Maggie was crying with relief but mostly with sorrow for my mum.

I was supposed to be safely tucked up in my bed when the verdict came through and Godfrey, Charlie and Dave all went down. Theresa and Evelyn were let off with a caution on account of being coerced, or something like that. Everyone was celebrating and, of course, I wasn't tucked up at all. I was in my usual position, earwigging on the stairs.

Then I heard Paulette's voice and my heart nearly stopped beating all over again. 'So, if that slimy git isn't Rosie's real dad, then who is?'

Great-aunt Dodie's voice rumbled across the ragged chorus of 'Who can say?' Actually, she said, she rather thought Cassandra could. They'd talked over the very matter and she was quite certain that Cassandra knew but simply wasn't telling. Not even to her favourite great-aunt.

By this time I was practically in the room, tongue hanging out, and I was able to catch a look that Auntie Maggie exchanged with Uncle Bert. It seemed very knowing, but they clamped their gobs shut and said nothing.

Soon after that, the party broke up and I was safely in bed when I heard Maggie and Bert climbing the stairs, whispering quietly.

'I know what you mean, Maggie, I caught the likeness too, just for a second. It was the way that doorway framed 'em when he was holding her. Still, it's likely we'll never know for sure. Probably best if we keep our thoughts on that particular subject under our hats. What d'you think, old girl, eh?'

I heard a slap and a giggle. 'Less of the "old", you. I'll have you know that I'm in my prime and don't you forget it.'

And Uncle Bert didn't forget it. None of us did; my auntie Maggie wouldn't let us. And we never forgot the summer of the Queen's Coronation either, or its ending. We celebrate what we call Rosie Day every year and everybody comes, including the man everyone thinks is my dad.

THE END

SEA OF DREAMS
by Susan Sallis

Holly and Mark Jepson have always spent Christmas on the Somerset coast, where Mark's uncle entertains a motley collection of guests in his holiday chalets. This year, they long to do something different – until uncle has to go into hospital, and they are obliged to put aside their plans for a quiet Christmas on their own. Instead they prepare to welcome the various members of the party – young and old, couples, children and old ladies, an eccentric artist and his handsome daughter (but is she *really* his daughter, the others wonder?), a young married pair expecting their first baby, to the secret envy of the childless Holly, and a wife escaping from a violent past. They are all, in their separate ways, to play a part in the unexpected, and at times shattering, events which take place before the new year dawns.

As the first fireworks of the year fall into the sea in a shower of silver stars, both guests and hosts at this wintry gathering look forward to a new and better world.

0 552 14867 9

THE COLOUR OF HOPE
by Susan Madison

All her life she had feared death by water . . .

Ruth Carter, her gentle husband Paul and their two children spend idyllic summers at their holiday retreat on the beautiful and rugged coast of Maine. But one year, as son Will celebrates his fourteenth birthday, a sailing trip goes tragically wrong and their beautiful, troubled daughter Josie is swept overboard. She disappears without trace.

Trapped in a spiral of guilt, grief and denial, Ruth finds her life beginning to fall apart. But fate has an even crueller trick up its sleeve, one which threatens to take from her everything that she holds most dear. The only thing she has to keep her going is hope – hope that a miracle will happen, hope that her family can rebuild their love for one another and recapture the joys of the past.

The Colour of Hope – a powerful and uplifting story of love, courage and hope for the future.

'An emotional roller-coaster of a novel, guaranteed to make you reach for your Kleenex'
Woman and Home

0 552 14772 9

THE BRASS DOLPHIN
by Caroline Harvey

Lila Cunningham, motherless since babyhood, was almost twenty-one when her familiar life in a small town on the Suffolk coast came abruptly to an end. It was 1938, and she learned with a shock that her endearing but feckless artist father faced financial disaster. With the loss of their home imminent, they had no option but to accept an offer of a house in Malta, and on that hot and exotic island, in the magnificent but crumbling Villa Zonda, Lila at last glimpsed the kind of life of which she had always dreamed.

But war was looming, and Malta became the focus of Hitler's attention while Lila became the focus of attention of three very different young men. As bombing devastated the island Lila, along with the other inhabitants, learned to live with privation and fear, and also to discover which dreams are really worth pursuing.

In this enchanting new novel Caroline Harvey captures all the warmth and romance of Malta as well as its dramatic sufferings during the Second World War.

Caroline Harvey is the pseudonym of the award-winning writer Joanna Trollope.

'The gorgeous exoticism of a Mediterranean island is masterfully conveyed'
Elizabeth Buchan, *The Times*

0 552 14553 X

THE SHADOW CHILD
by Judith Lennox

July 1914, the eve of the First World War, and fourteen-year-old Alix Gregory is holidaying in France with the wealthy Lanchbury family. She is looking after two-year-old Charlie Lanchbury when he disappears during a family picnic and is never seen again. Once a happy, reckless girl, Alix is blamed for the tragedy and cannot escape from the resulting disintegration of the family.

The war ends and Alix tries to pick up the threads of her life. Through marriage and the birth of her son, Rory, she finds happiness, and through her meeting with the brothers Derry and Jonathan Fox, she finds love. Yet, living in her ancient and beautiful home, Owlscote, she is haunted by the loss of her baby cousin. As the years pass, and as the world descends into the horrors of war once more, the question remains: will Charlie Lanchbury ever be found?

In *The Shadow Child* Judith Lennox has written her most brilliant and touching novel, a story of love and loss that stays forever in the mind.

0 552 14603 X

HEART OF A WARRIOR
by Johanna Lindsey

A love that is written in the stars . . .

Brittany is proud and strong, a modern woman who vows that no man will ever plumb the depths of her soul. Then one day, Dalden walks into her life. She sees him across the lawn, where he immediately entices her with his tremendous strength and physical presence. Dalden is a warrior, powerful and brave, a man who fearlessly fights for what he wants. And he wants Brittany . . .

He begs her to help him in his quest. It is a quest which will take Brittany to strange new worlds – and the depths of her own heart.

'First-rate romance'
New York Daily News

0 552 14912 8

A SELECTED LIST OF FINE NOVELS
AVAILABLE FROM CORGI BOOKS

THE PRICES SHOWN BELOW WERE CORRECT AT THE TIME OF GOING TO PRESS. HOWEVER TRANSWORLD PUBLISHERS RESERVE THE RIGHT TO SHOW NET RETAIL PRICES ON COVERS WHICH MAY DIFFER FROM THOSE PREVIOUSLY ADVERTISED IN THE TEXT OR ELSEWHERE.

All Transworld titles are available by post from:
Bookpost, PO Box 29, Douglas, Isle of Man IM99 1BQ
Credit cards accepted. Please telephone 01624 836000,
fax 01624 837033, Internet http://www.bookpost.co.uk or
e-mail: bookshop@enterprise.net for details.
Free postage and packing in the UK.
Overseas customers allow £1 per book.